Cupid

JAHQUEL J.

Copyright © 2023
Published by Jahquel J.
www.Jahquel.com
ALL RIGHTS RESERVED
Any unauthorized reprint or use of the material is prohibited. No part of this book may be reproduced or transmitted in any form or by any means, electronic, or mechanical, including photocopying, recording, or by any information storage without express permission by the publisher. This is an original work of fiction. Name, characters, places, and incident are either products of the author's imagination or are used fictitiously and any resemblance to actual persons, living or dead is entirely coincidental. Contains explicit languages and adult themes. suitable for ages 16+

Jahquel J's Catalog

Series:
In Love With The King Of Harlem 1-5
To All The Thugs I loved That Didn't Love Me Back 1-4
Never Wanted To Be Wifey 1-2
Crack Money With Cocaine Dreams 1-2
All The Dope Boys Gon Feel Her 1-2
Good Girls Love Hustlas 1-3
I Got Nothing But Love For My Hitta 1-2
She Ain't Never Met A N*gga Like Me 1-3
A Staten Island Love Letter 1-5
Married To A Brownsville Bully 1-3

BAE: Before Anyone Else 1-3
Ghetto Love Birds
Homies, Lovers + Friends 1-5
Confessions Of A Hustla's Housekeeper 1-3
Thugs Need Love 1-3

Spin-offs:
In Love With An East Coast Maniac 1-3
A Staten Island Love Affair 1-3
A Brownsville, Harlem + Staten Island Holiday Affair
Rose In Harlem: Harlem King's Princess
She Never Had A Nigga Like Me: Beto & Keka
Confessions Of A Hustla's Daughter

Standalones:

I Can't Be The One You Love
I'm Riding With You Forever
Forever, I'm Ready

Emotionless
It's Always Been You, Baby Girl
Homies, Lovers + Wives: A Homies, Lovers + Friends Spin-off.
Cupid

Synopsis:

Madison Shaw is the new teacher at Brookwood elementary school. She moved from New York to Brookwood, North Carolina after ending a three-year relationship. New to town, she spends her days teaching and nights snuggled up with wine and her favorite book.

During a parent-teacher conference she meets Parker Woods, her favorite student's father. It takes one look for Angel to see that his father is smitten by his teacher. Parker Woods is a newly divorced single dad. His divorce from Angel's mom was tough on him. He's not interested in dating, though his ex has remarried. When he meets Madison Shaw, he feels his heart beating again.

The idea of dating and love scares both Parker and Madison. However, the heart always knows what's best. Will these two end up together? Or will their broken hearts remain broken?

**Kali, New Jersey + Brookwood, North Carolina are fictional cities in this book. **

1: Parker Woods

I watched my ex-wife kiss and hug our son before he ran over toward me. We had been meeting in this Walmart parking lot since he was five years old. Like clockwork, every week we would make the switch. She'd fill me in on anything that I needed to know, and I'd do the same. Angel threw himself into my arms and I hugged him while he looked up at me. I had missed the past two swaps because I was out of town for work. My job was working on merging with another company in Houston, and I had been sent out there to overlook everything that needed to be looked over. I hated being away from my son. Luckily, me and my ex-wife, Luna, had a great relationship and she knew how to hold down the fort when I couldn't be there.

"I missed you so much, Dad," he beamed as he looked up into my eyes. "Do you know I tossed the winning basket at the game last weekend?" he continued on.

Angel Parker was my entire world. I loved being a father more than being a human. He was my reason and the air that filled my lungs every day. It was the only reason I worked as hard as I did. Angel deserved the world, and I would die giving it to him.

"I heard, Pop. Mom sent me the video when I was in Houston," I informed him. "We can watch it together before bed tonight," I promised him.

"Yesss!" He jumped up and down while doing a dance he probably learned on Fortnite.

"Go and buckle yourself in while I talk to your mama real quick."

"Yes sir," he replied and hopped off toward my car a few feet away. I chuckled and walked over toward where his mother was standing.

Even with us being divorced for five years, I couldn't deny the fact that Luna looked good. She was a spit fire Latina with strong opinions and an even stronger right hook. Her tanned golden skin glistened under the February sun while she stood in her Nike leggings and sports bra. More than likely, she was going to the gym as soon as she left here.

"What's up, Luna?"

"Hey Mr. Parkerrrr," she laughed, and we shared a brief hug. "How does it feel to be back home?"

"Good. I was tired of eating out all the time."

"I see," she eyed my stomach. "Looking like you packed some weight on too."

"I mean, we all can't look like you," I smirked. "On the real, I appreciate you holding it down for me while I handled work obligations."

Whenever Luna smiled, she exposed that left cheek dimple that I loved so much. Whenever she made that face, she could get whatever she wanted from me. Which is what she did when she came sliding in our house with Target bags. It was also the same smirk I had grown to despise when we were going through our divorce. It took a lot for us to get here, and I thanked God that we were here.

"You need to start joining me. I go around this time almost every day."

"Nah, you not about to have me screaming and shit... How's the fiancé?"

She smiled. "Dexter is good. We're actually going cake tasting this week while Angel is with you."

"Nice. Make sure you pick out something that's not chocolate," I poked fun at her. Luna had picked out chocolate cake for our wedding and complained the whole night because she kept having to wipe her teeth clean from the chocolate.

"I'm much more experienced these days, and my palette has changed quite a bit. Did you receive your save the date?"

"It's probably on my kitchen table somewhere. I haven't had the chance to go through my mail since I got home."

"Hmm. Okay. Angel really wants you there to see him walk down the aisle. You know... since we got married before he was born."

"He never lets us forget it." Angel has held a grudge with us since he found out that we got married before he was born.

Luna giggled. "Dexter has mentioned he would love for you to be there when he's fitted for his suit," she mentioned.

Dexter was a cool dude and I respected how much he made it a point to include my son in everything with this wedding.

He was the one who wanted to meet me before he even met Angel. It was important to him to get my blessing when it came to entering my son's life. Luna and Dexter had been dating for a full year before Angel even met him.

"For sure. Let him know that I appreciate him including me in all of this." It made me emotional thinking about my son having another male figure in his life.

"Of course." She turned and headed toward the driver side of her car. "Don't forget that Angel has his teacher conferences too. His teacher mentioned he has been a little bit talkative lately."

"Noted. See you next week... unless you want to let me make my two weeks I missed."

"I'll let you know by the middle of this week." She winked and got into her car. I shook my head and headed toward mine.

Angel had already pulled out his tablet and was consumed with whatever You-

Tube video he was watching. I knew better than to try and make conversation with him whenever he was like that. I got a bunch of one word answers and head nods whenever he was tuned in with that damn tablet. At times I hated that I even bought it for his birthday last year. Luna had always been on a no technology kick when he was younger. Now I understood why she was so pissed when I surprised him with it at his birthday party last year. Dexter was the one who came to my defense by showing Luna all the educational shit he could do on the tablet. Even though we knew Angel wasn't going to pay attention to none of those apps we downloaded on there.

    Luna was lucky to have met a man like Dexter after our divorce. At least she had been able to open her heart up again and truly love. All I had been granted with was a bunch of one night stands and meaningless follow up text messages. After the way the last year of our marriage had been' I wasn't sure if I ever wanted to date again. I was cool with not getting into anything serious. Luna on the other hand threw herself back into dating. The minute our names were signed onto the divorce papers was the moment that Luna signed up for all the dating sites that she could. I wasn't mad at her either. Toward the end of our marriage, I had mentally and physically checked out from her.

We had gotten married so young that neither of us knew what we were getting into. Me and Luna had always known the same people and ran in the same circles. It wasn't strange to run into her at different kickbacks around the hood. Whenever we ran into each other we would always flirt with one another. It was clear that the attraction was there between us. We just never spent enough time with each other to know if we clicked emotionally. Not until we attended her cousin's birthday party. Luna showed up with her boyfriend at the time and I showed up alone. I didn't even want to show up because I had just gotten off work an hour before the party. Luna's cousin, Cam, begged me to come by to show my face and get a plate of food. Home cooked food wasn't coming around often, so I wasn't going to give up the chance to scoop a plate and drop a card off for Cam.

Soon as I pulled up, I saw Luna arguing with her boyfriend. He tossed her purse onto the grass and pulled off without her. From the way she was going off I knew she was done with the nigga. Luna and her cousins were known for being stuck up bitches. Every guy I knew that had tried to hit always said that they thought they were too good. Luna and her cousin had goals and those guys weren't used to being with girls like them. I always respected Cam and Luna from the way they carried themselves. After the party I offered to drive

Luna back to the dorms. From the moment her butt sat in my passenger seat I knew that she would be my wife.

I proposed to Luna at our graduation. Neither of us knew what we were doing or what was next for us. The one thing we did know was that we wanted to be together. When I proposed I figured we would remain engaged for a few years and then plan our dream wedding. Both of us were college graduates with a mountain of debt. Luna was going to law school which was more debt, and I had gotten a job on a sales team at a very lucrative pharmaceutical company. Having a wedding wasn't on any of our agendas. Luna got accepted into a law school in North Carolina. Our parents wanted us to get married before moving there. Luckily, my company had an office down here, so I was able to transfer.

Me and Luna were from a small town in Kali, New Jersey. It was a small town twenty minutes from New York City.

Everybody knew everyone. Even though we went to school an hour away from our hometown, our families had always known one another. While we wanted to wait to get married our family had a different plan. Luna's mother started planning the wedding soon as she revealed the news. It wasn't like any of us could tell them no. They agreed to pay for the wedding and give us money for a down payment on our first home. Knowing the amount of debt we were in from school, and me only starting my career, I knew it was best to shut up and let them take the lead.

Hindsight, I wished that we would have just did our own thing. Because we were so caught up in giving our families what they wanted, we never had a chance to think about what we wanted. If we had it our way we wouldn't have gotten married right away. Whenever I sat and thought about how stressed we were because of that wedding, I always regret not putting my foot down and telling our parents no. It was hard having to deal with a wedding while moving to a new state. At least I had it easier than Luna. Between her mother and mine they called and bothered Luna on the daily basis. All I was responsible for was requesting time off from work and making sure my suit fit.

After our wedding we settled in Brookwood, North Carolina. With the help of our family we were able to purchase a two bedroom, one and a half bath house in a diverse neighborhood. Our first few years of marriage was a blur for us. I was working so much and Luna was so busy with law school that neither of us made our marriage a priority. We had this nagging voice in the back of our heads telling us that we had to make it. Both of our parents had put so much pressure on us that we had no choice but to be great in whatever we did. Within two years I had been promoted to a better paying position. It helped take some of the pressure off of us.

Just when we were finding a groove and making time for our marriage Luna found out she was pregnant. The pregnancy resulted in a miscarriage. I hated that I felt relieved. Luna, on the other hand was distraught. It took her some time to get over it, and even then I don't think she ever got over it completely. Something changed in her that night at the hospital. Our conversations went from where we should travel when we had the time, and what international city we wanted to live in for the summer, to talking about babies and starting to convert our second bedroom from my office to a nursery. Babies were on her mind often and I just wasn't there yet. My career was considered my baby and I wasn't ready to become a father to a human child. It's funny because when I look at Angel, I can't imagine my life without him. He's the air in my lungs and

I'd do anything that I could for that little boy.

Luna eventually graduated law school and then passed the bar. She was able to get a job at a law firm here in town. We spent our days building our careers and our nights trying to recover from the long work days. There wasn't any romance from either party. We lived two different lives under the same roof. We tried therapy for a while and that just turned into us pointing the finger at each other. The problem was that we were never trying to fix our marriage because of us. It was always about our parents. We didn't want to disappoint them by divorcing, so we stuck it out. When Luna got pregnant with Angel, I thought this was our chance. It was our chance to make this right for our son.

For a while we did good. Our distraction used to be work and now it was Angel. He needed us around the clock. Luna had taken maternity leave, and I was still working the long hours. Her mother flew down to stay with us until Angel was three months. Once she left it was like the rug was pulled from underneath us. Luna had become resentful of me working long hours. There was always an argument about something. I could never come home to a nice conversation and a glass of wine. Yeah, it wasn't ideal when you practically had a newborn. I never had a problem getting up in the middle of the night or jumping in as soon as I came in from work. Luna wouldn't allow me to do anything.

When I came in from work Angel had already had his bath and was asleep. In the middle of the night when he whined she would jump up and use breastfeeding as an excuse. I understood breastfeeding our son was the best. At times I felt like she used it to hurt me. Since she hated that I worked so much, she wanted to make an example and that was making sure I didn't get the chance to bond with my son. Eventually I started to take personal days and get off at a more reasonable hour. The tension seemed to settle down for a bit.

I can say that we tried to make it work. Despite both being miserable, we tried to make our marriage work for our son. My parents had been together since college and were happily married. I was raised in a house filled with love. My parents never spoke ill of each other and they never fought in front of us kids. Everyday they decided to choose each other and that's what I did. I wasn't happy in my marriage and knew we should have just called it quits. That small voice in the back of my head always told me to keep pushing forward. Luna was my wife and I needed to constantly choose my wife. With Angel in the picture it made it even more difficult to leave. While I was feeling like this, Luna was feeling the exact same way. She was tired and wanted to throw in the towel a few times.

Once we decided to quit lying to ourselves, we realized that our son deserved happy parents. He didn't want an overly stressed mother or a father that took on extra hours to avoid being under the same roof for long periods of time. Angel deserved parents that smiled when their feet hit the floor each morning. It took six months for us to come clean to our parents. Instead of being angry they apologized to us. They realized they had played a part in our divorce by speeding up our marriage. We never got the chance to live before being tied down by marriage. Our parents gave us their blessing to divorce and chase happiness – whatever that means.

Within a month of telling our parents I was moving out into my own condo. In our divorce, I decided to let Luna keep the house. Angel already had to deal with the reality that his parents weren't together anymore. He shouldn't have to give up everything that he's familiar with. We agreed to split custody of our son. The one thing we always agreed on was that we were great parents and never wanted to take our bitterness out on our child's time with one another. We alternated weeks and holidays. Angel would be with me one week and then his mother the next week. I eventually moved from my condo into a townhouse that was ten minutes from Luna and right in the middle of Angel's school. Whenever he was over my house he was still able to hang out with his friends that lived over by his mother's house. We wanted to keep things as normal as possible.

"Daddy, do you hear me?"

Angel snapped me out of my trip down memory hell. "Nah, what's up, Pop?"

"Can we go out to eat tonight? Mom is all about only cooking what's in the house," he cut his eyes at the thought of his mother's healthy lifestyle.

Luna had become heavily into fitness after our divorce. She said it took her mind off everything we were going through at the time. While she found solace in fitness, I had found peace in working. I didn't have anybody hounding me because I worked late. It was like heaven coming home to quiet without having Luna being passive aggressive toward me.

"Daddddd!"

"Yeah, we can grab something to eat," I chuckled.

He was satisfied with my answer so he went back to his tablet. I shook my head and made a right to head to his favorite restaurant – *Red Lobster*.

2: Madison Shaw

"Your profile is so boring, Madison," Ericka, my best friend, insulted my dating profile. "Blah, she's a teacher, blah she loves wine. Blah, blah, blah," she continued picking apart my profile I spent two weeks putting together.

"I am not boring," I defended and took a sip of my drink. Luckily, it wasn't wine or Ericka would have had a field day.

Ericka heaved a sigh and stared at me. "This is the exact reason I wanted to come visit you here. You tell me everything is amazing and I'm not too sure."

"Everything is amazing. I have my peace back and I'm enjoying getting to know the city."

"This small ass city, Madison. Why did you even accept this job?" Ericka looked down at her phone. "Give me a second, I have to take this one."

"Sure." I took another sip of my drink and watched as she shuffled toward the exit to take a call.

Ericka was a therapist and had been my best friend since third grade. Every major loss or gain I celebrated she had been there for. I was there when she pushed my goddaughter out, and there when she had to bury her dog of fifteen years. Our friendship was more like a sisterhood. She was the only person who could be brutally honest with me and live to talk about it. I knew the moment I boarded the flight with a one-way ticket she was worried. Brooklyn, New York had always been home to me. I never thought I would move away. After my stepfather passed, I thought my mother was crazy for moving to Florida. For sure I thought she had lost her mind and needed to find it in Florida before coming to her senses and coming home.

"Sorry about that. I left a entire list for Mitch and he's still confused about *our* daughter." She rolled her eyes and sat her phone back down on the table.

"That's your husband."

"And I love him dearly. Sometimes I just want to strangle him and then ride his dick at the Sam—"

"Mitch is like a brother to me and I don't want to hear about you fucking him... eww," I laughed and pushed my empty glass to the front of the table.

"Red Lobster is the fanciest restaurant in this town?" Ericka looked around the casual family-friendly restaurant.

"Can you quit? I happen to love the drinks here and their crab dip is one of my favorites." There were thousands of Red Lobster restaurants everywhere. This one was family owned and you could tell they put a little bit more love into their food. Every time I came here I was always impressed by the drinks and food. "Stop acting like we didn't eat here all the time in college."

"Yeah, we're grown ass women now. There's nothing wrong with Red Lobster, Maddie. I can have this at home... I wanted you to show me Brookwood."

"This is Brookwood. Everyone comes here after a stressful work day. We have other fancier restaurants, but considering we're both dressed in workout gear I chose this place." We had just finished a five-mile hike in the woods. It was one of my favorite things to do now that I was a resident of Brookwood.

"Why do you want to live here?" It was the question she had been dying to ask since I picked her up from the airport a few days ago.

"Ericka, it's not that bad here. Yes, it's different from what we're used to. I have come to love the small town life."

"Girl, this is not a Hallmark movie and you're not the leading character in distress. Selling your Brooklyn condo and nearly half your things and then buying a one-way ticket is a midlife crisis, and you're not even midlife yet," she took a bite of their biscuits and leaned back.

"When you decided to move to New Jersey to be closer to Mitch I supported you. I never made you feel like your decision was a bad one. Instead I encouraged you, and I just want you to do the same. I needed something different and this happened to be it. Case closed."

Ericka looked away. "I'm sorry, Maddie. I know I haven't been the most supportive when it came to this move."

"You haven't and I allowed you to sulk

and have your way. Joshua nearly pulled my heart out of my chest when he called off the wedding. How can I continue to live in that condo knowing what we shared there? I just needed something new, E."

She reached across the table and grabbed my hands. "I know and I'm a selfish bitch."

"This is true." We both broke out in laughter because it was true. Ericka always meant well, however, she was selfish too. This move was more about her than me. Who would she have Tuesday margaritas with and she and Mitch were losing their free babysitter.

"Have you reached out to him since moving here?"

"Nope. I blocked him on social media and his phone number. I'm trying to push forward and don't need him stalling that process."

"I'm proud of you."

When Joshua decided to call off the

wedding a week before I thought my life was over. How could you do something like that? I asked and begged him if this was what he wanted. He insisted that I was the only woman for him and he'd marry me over and over again if he could. After giving an answer like that, who would second guess? I was certain that I would have been Mrs. Madison Clemons by now. Instead, I was bitter, angry and living in a different state.

"Thank you," I smiled.

How do you end a three-year relationship in one weekend? It was a question that I continued to torture myself with. I wanted to know what made a person just want to give up? Why walk away from someone who you have a future with? Me and Joshua had planned everything from our wedding down to where we would raise children. Everything was mapped out perfectly, even the golden doodle puppy he surprised me with for our third anniversary we had just celebrated a week before he decided to bust up our life.

At least he was considerate, right? He allowed me to keep our condo that we purchased together. Both Ericka and my mother thought I was crazy when I told them we were purchasing a home together. They warned me to wait until after he proposed to me. Silly me. I couldn't wait and jumped in head first. Love was always a weakness for me. Whenever I was in love I was downright silly and all about the person I was dating. Despite being hurt in the past, whenever I was in a relationship I was all in. It was because I truly believed in *love*. When two people who are meant to be came together it was special. It's supposed to feel like no other feeling in the entire world. It doesn't matter if you had love with someone else. This feeling doesn't feel like any other feeling that you've felt with someone else.

What made our breakup worst was the

fact that I had to walk into my classroom filled with students and tell them I wasn't getting married anymore. They were all invited to the wedding and had been working on a song with the music teacher for me and Joshua. I think that hurt more than calling my mother and telling her to cancel her plane ticket. Me and my mother sat on the phone sobbing for what could have been. I think she was more excited about welcoming a new family member into our lives. It had always been just the three of us – my mother, stepfather and me. We didn't have much family, and after Paul, my stepfather, died it was just me and my mother. The thought of having new family members entering our lives was enough to brighten our entire year.

"Ms. Shaw!" a semi-familiar voice called from behind me. I slowly turned around and smiled when I saw Angel sitting there. "Dad, this is my favorite teacher."

"Um, I think I'm your only teacher. How are you, Angel," I smiled at him. Angel Woods was such a sweet, beautiful child. From his behavior I could tell that he was well loved at home.

"Yeah... that's true. Ms. Shaw, why are you here?"

That was when, I assumed, his father stepped in with a chuckle. "Teachers gotta eat too, Pop." He was sitting in the booth closest to me. "How are you? Parker Woods," he introduced himself while extending his hand.

"Hi, Mr. Woods. I'm Angel's new teacher... Madison Shaw." My hand slipped into his smooth and strong hand perfectly. "Actually we're supposed to meet this week."

"Oh that's right." Angel's father was gorgeous. Since it was still the beginning of the school year I was still learning about the students and their parents. If I had to assume Mr. Wood's occupation I would have marked model. "I hope to hear nothing but good news, right?" he side eyed Angel who was smiling widely.

"Angel is one of my best students, Mr. Woods," I smirked.

"Parker... just call me Parker. Woods seems so formal."

"Well, Parker," I smiled. "Enjoy your dinner and I will see you and your wife this week," I tried to turn around, but Angel stopped me.

"My mommy and daddy are divorced," he blurted.

"Oh. Lucky you... that means two times the presents for Christmas," I quickly recovered. "Enjoy your dinner and I'll see you tomorrow."

Angel smiled and went back to finishing his dinner with his father. When I turned back around Ericka had apparently been burning a hole in the back of my neck. "Bitch," she whispered.

I motioned for her to be quiet and

waved the waiter over for the check. We had been here for quite some time and I didn't want to polish off anymore drinks with my student seated a few feet away. We settled our check and then headed out to grab milkshakes before returning back to my place.

"You can't tell me that he didn't play on P-valley. That's Diamond, bitch," she hollered the moment we got into the car.

I laughed because the two did resemble each other. He could have been his brother. "Oh shut up."

"A divorced single father... girl, I see why you moved to this small ass town."

I rolled my eyes and headed toward the ice cream shop. "Ericka, I didn't move here for a man. In fact, I moved here to get away from a damn man."

"All I'm saying is that he's fine as hell and from the way he rubbed the back of your hand he thinks the same as you. Whew, he was fineeee!" She fanned herself and let the window down at the same time.

It wasn't unfamiliar to run into one of my students in town. The city wasn't that big, and everybody had to eat – right? Since I was new here I hadn't formally met any of the parents. They had received the letter from the school about me becoming a new fourth grade teacher at Brookwood elementaryschool. Other than that I hadn't had a chance to learn who was who, and which parents were divorced. I tuned Ericka out as she went on and on about how the fine men were hidden away in Brookwood. I had a rule on dating my student's parents. Even if I thought Parker Woods was fine, I would never act on it. Plus, I needed to rid my heart of Joshua before even thinking about moving on with someone else.

3: Parker Woods

"Welcome back to the office. I was getting a little lonely with you being gone," Tracy, my best friend, said while leaning on my office door.

Me and Tracy started at the same time and kicked in doors at this company. At the time we were the only brothers here and were determined to kick down every door to advance to where we were now. We both started out in sales and now we were heading a new department dedicated to a new merger from a company we had acquired. I made a great salary with benefits and that's all I had ever wanted. My father always instilled having a great career that I enjoyed. Not going to college wasn't an option for me and my siblings. Our parents believed you got further with a degree. When I was younger I didn't believe them. College was stupid to me and I would have much rather travel with my friends.

As an adult, I was grateful to them for forcing me to go to college. Yeah, I had a bunch of debit that I spent years working to clear. In the end, if I hadn't got a degree I wouldn't have been able to afford to pay them in the first place. My parents did help and pay at least five thousand dollars per sibling. The moment they found out they were pregnant with each of my siblings, they put money away for college. School was important to my parents. It was what they stressed all throughout raising us. My younger sister, Francis, didn't understand how important it was to them. When she graduated from high school she moved abroad to France. My parents thought it was so she could study abroad. Franny moved to France for love and never looked back at the states. She came for the holidays and always left behind her mysterious lover. We didn't know what Franny did for a living, all we knew is that she never held her hand out asking for anything.

"I'm happy to be back in my own bed. Was tired of staying from hotel-to-hotel while being there," I admitted.

Going out of town for work was never easy. I missed out on spending time with Angel and I was away from my routine. I enjoyed my home and loved sleeping on my expensive mattress. The mattresses in different hotels never felt the same to me.

"Angel missed you too. Luna let me take him out for dinner last week." Tracy was Angel's godfather. From the moment we started working together we just clicked. He knew just how hard me and Luna worked at our marriage. Some of our lunches were spent with me venting and trying to seek advice.

"Oh yeah? She didn't tell me. Where did he make you bring him?" I asked already knowing the place.

"Red Lobster." Tracy laughed. "He even finessed the waitress to bring him a to-go box filled with them damn biscuits. He's going to turn into a biscuit if he doesn't quit."

I laughed. Angel was obsessed with Red Lobster and everything it had to offer. "How's Mari doing?"

Tracy smiled. "Real good."

"Have you guys finalized the wedding yet?"

Tracy and Mari from Human Resources had been together for two years. Tracy always flirted with her, then again, he flirted with everybody. I didn't think he was serious until he told me he asked her out. Since they were from two different departments their relationship wasn't forbidden. All they had to do was make the company aware of their relationship. Valentine's Day last year was when he asked Mari to marry him. That was when they started planning their wedding. I'm not going to lie, the sound of wedding planning still gave me hives. It left a bad taste in my mouth and further reminded me why I was still single and I wasn't looking.

"Mari is forever adding more shit to the wedding. She promised that the sparklers were the last damn thing."

"I told you all about that wedding planning stuff. It's the Super Bowl for women," I shook my head and replied to an email.

Tracy looked over at me. "Her best

friend is coming into town to see her dress. It might be good to ask her out. You're the best man and she's the maid of honor."

"No."

Tracy stepped into my office and closed the door behind him. "Come on, Parker. Jada is a good one," he vouched for Mari's best friend. "She has her own business, home an—"

"And lives in Atlanta. How is that ever going to work? I'm not moving for a relationship. I couldn't do that to Angel."

The one thing me and Luna promised each other was that we would never leave Brookwood. If we found love and it took us away from Brookwood, then we wouldn't go through with it. When she met Dexter, he was from Virginia. He moved to Brookwood to be with her. *If* I decided to open my heart up to another woman, she would have to move here to be with me. Angel had just got used to his parents not being together, and I refused to move away from him. Atlanta was a few hours away and something that was doable if I did decide to move away. Except, I would miss out on my son's life. On weeks that I didn't have Angel, I could always pop by his basketball practice or Luna's house to see him.

It took a long time for us to develop that kind of relationship. Now that we had it, I wouldn't do anything to jeopardize it. "Maybe she'd be willing to live here. Her best friend is here after all."

"Jada has a successful salon and life in Atlanta. She's not giving that up for nobody. I'd rather not get involved with something that has no future. She's a cute girl."

"*She's a cute girl,*" Tracy mocked. "Man, you need to get back out there. Luna is getting remarried and you're still twiddling your thumbs."

"I have meaningful relationships with the women I know."

"Yeah, sending them on their way after you pound their guts in," I choked on the coffee I just took a sip of.

"Trace, you serious right now," I grabbed napkins and wiped my mouth before the coffee could fall on my Tom Ford blazer.

Tracy laughed. "I mean, sex isn't a relationship. Tell me I'm wrong."

"You're not wrong. I'm not ready for something serious right now. Right now isn't the time to have a relationship."

"When is the time?"

A light tap interrupted a question I didn't want to answer. Greg, our coworker, popped his head in. "We on for lunch today?"

"Yeah. I was actually finishing up some stuff. Meet you down in the parking garage," I told him.

When the door closed I laughed at Tracy's face. "When the fuck you started having lunch with Greg?"

"When we had to spend all that time together in Houston. Remember you couldn't go because you had to do wedding tasting with Mari?" I powered my computer off and stood up. "He's cool though. Come out with us."

"I wish I could. Mari is using every second of my life to plan something. She wants to look at the floral arrangements, and the shop happens to be fifteen minutes from here."

"Good luck, bro'," I tapped his shoulder and headed out of my office.

As much as Mari stressed him out about this wedding, I knew he would do it over again in a heartbeat. That was just how much he loved her. It differed from me and Luna's wedding. We were forced to get married and having a wedding planned for us. Mari and Tracy's wedding was on their terms. Neither of their parents or friends were involved. The only thing I was responsible for was planning a bachelor party that would put all others to shame.

* * *

I rushed into Brookwood elementary school like I had the devil on the heels of my loafers. We had been to the school during open school week so I knew where Angel's class was. Since it was parent-teacher conference the students were able to stay until their parent showed. I was fifteen minutes late for my designated time and I hated to be late. Even with Brookwood having the small town feel, traffic around this time was out of control. When people heard of a small town that Black folks are doing well in, they naturally gravitated toward it.

"I'm sorry. Sorry," I busted into the classroom where Angel and Ms. Shaw were sitting at her desk.

The two of them were playing Uno

and sharing pretzels. "Dad, you're late. We're always supposed to be early... never late," Angel recited what I had always instilled into him. Positivity always came out of being early. Nobody was ever positive when someone was late.

"Sorry, Pop... traffic was crazy in Brook Square. Ms. Shaw, my apologies about being late."

She smiled and wiped the pretzel crumbs off her hands. "I know firsthand how much traffic accumulates into Brook Square. I've been caught in it more than a few times." Her toffee-colored complexion glistened when the sunlight coming in from the windows hit her.

She wore a pair of pink cropped dress pants, penny loafers and silk green shirt. Her curly hair was pushed up into a bun with only a few curls loose. "I remember a time when it didn't get the crowded. All these new folks moving here and making traffic worse."

"New folks like me?" she raised her eyebrow at me. I wanted to lift my size twelve foot and put it into my mouth. "Mr. Woods, I'm joking with you. Come and take a seat," she waved for me to sit.

"Does this mean that I have to sit in the cafeteria with everyone else?"

Ms. Shaw smiled and gently touched his cheek. "Unfortunately, it does. I promise we will finish this game tomorrow at lunch."

Angel must have been satisfied with his answer because he grabbed his book bag and skipped on out the door. "He's a character."

"Yes, he is. A good one. You and his mother do such a great job with him. I've had plenty of divorced children in my classes in the past and you can always tell."

"I'll take that as a compliment. Our biggest goal was to make sure that Angel never suffers."

She pulled his file from a drawer in her

desk and looked at it before speaking. I watched as she removed that curly fine strand out of her face. Her sweet fragrance tickled my nose and turned me on at the same time.

"I love when parents can come together for the greater good of their child," she commented. "Angel is a great student. I love having him in my class and he's so smart. I noticed when going over his file that he does have an IEP."

"Yes. He struggled a bit when he started school. They diagnosed him with a specific learning disability."

"I saw that. His IEP meeting is coming up so we don't need to get into specifics here. He does get taken out of the class for certain lessons, and a secondary teacher joins us as well some days. Angel is doing wonderful with keeping up with the speed of the class, and he's so helpful, too."

"Does he struggle at times?"

"He does. However, he's not afraid to

speak up and let me or Mrs. Humming know that he's struggling."

I blew a sigh of relief. Angel struggled throughout first and second grade. Naturally, we thought he was acting out because of his home life. We learned that he chose to act out in class because he didn't understand the work and was struggling hard. Once we figured out what was going on, the school district jumped into action and requested the additional help he would need. An IEP is a individualized education program, which is a piece of paper that helps children with learning disabilities. The paper tracks everything from when the child started receiving different services until high school.

Luna cried when we found out Angel would be receiving special education services. To us, special-ed meant something different. We grew up with kids being bullied because of it. As an adult, we learned so much and how different it was from when we were children. Once we were educated we stood ten toes behind Angel and his school. Whatever they recommended we took into consideration and applied it to Angel.

"Good. I know in third grade he had a problem asking for help."

"I noticed Angel doesn't have many friends. The other boys in class often make fun of him so he eats lunch alone most days."

I sighed. "He had the same problem last year with those same boys."

"Another teacher filled me in. I started having lunch with Angel myself and we've become quite the Uno gamblers," she covered her mouth while she giggled.

"So you're the reason he's always raising me a Snicker bar?"

"Guilty," her smile was so contagious. I couldn't help but to crack a smile each time she did. "He's really a great kid and I enjoy spending time with him. You and his mother have done a wonderful job with him."

Angel is and will always be my biggest flex. He was the one thing that me and Luna agreed on. Everything else we didn't agree on, but Angel was that one thing we never had any arguments about.

"I appreciate that. Me and my ex-wife are always on the same page when it comes to Angel."

"That's great. Angel is truly an angel in my class and I have no complaints with him. Other than I've been buying a bunch of Snicker bars lately," she giggled again.

"That's good to hear. I'll make sure to inform his mother too."

"Amazing."

"How are you settling in here? The school notice they sent out stated that you were from New York."

She closed Angel's file and put it back into her desk. "It's a slower pace that I'm enjoying. When I lived in New York I felt like I lived to work. Moving here, I can actually enjoy my career and have a life too. Even though I don't have much of a life... other than my wine and books," she muttered.

"I know you're not home drinking wine and reading books when you can be exploring the city?"

"Well, not right now. My best friend is in town so she's been dragging me all over. Once she leaves tomorrow I'll return back to wine, books and binge-watching Netflix."

I was curious to know more about Madison Shaw. "I would love to take you out and show you Brookwood."

From her facial expression I could tell that she was taken aback. Hell, I was taken back by my own bluntness. Usually I would have listened to her report on Angel and moved on. Sitting here with her and listening to how much she adored my son made me want to get to know her more.

All the teachers at Brookwood elementary were amazing teachers. The vibe just felt different when it came to Ms. Shaw.

"Mr. Woods, I have a rule on not dating my student's parents."

"Who said that this was a date? I'm a parent that just wants to show my son's teacher a great time around Brookwood."

I could tell that she was thinking about it. "Hmm, I guess we can get something on the books."

"See! That's the spirit, Ms. Shaw."

"Madison, please," she corrected me.

I stood up and shook her hand. "I'll be in touch about our little tour guide outing," I chuckled, which caused her to giggle. A giggle I had come to adore in the fifteen minutes that we've been seated together.

"Looking forward to it. Tell Angel that I'll see him tomorrow," she smiled as I headed toward the door.

"Will do. Have a great day, Ms. Shaw."

"Madison!" she corrected and sat down to prepare for the next parents that were going to come through her door. I hadn't been this excited about a woman in a while.

4: Madison Shaw

When Parker Woods rushed into my classroom fifteen minutes late this afternoon, I didn't expect him to volunteer to show me around Brookwood. The night we met at Red Lobster I knew he was a fine specimen of a man. Ericka did everything except hollering it out in the restaurant. It wasn't like Parker Woods was the first sexy parent I had come across. Brookwood was filled with successful Black men that happened to all have kids. Even on the dating site the majority of men here had children and had experienced marriage already.

I guess at thirty-three I had to understand that the majority of men had already been married and had children. It was me who was single and child-less. It was discouraging when I saw my friends with their children or husbands. I swiped through social media and saw constant pregnancy announcements or engagement pictures. Then I opened the mail and had save the dates, and I was no closer to any of those things. For a while I considered if I wanted to freeze my eggs. Maybe my happily ever after didn't look like everyone else's. Joshua promised that we would get married and then start working on having kids. Now I was single and living in a new state without him. Whenever I put my trust into a man I was always the one who ended up looking stupid.

"My bag better not be overweight either," Ericka shoved her bag closed while struggling to zip it.

"With all the shopping you were doing

at the outlets I wouldn't be surprised if it was," I laughed while going over the lesson plans for tomorrow's lessons. If that wasn't enough, I was emailing the three sets of parents who couldn't make the conferences.

Ericka gave up on shoving her bag closed and plopped down on the edge of my bed. "What are you over there working on?"

"Work. I have to reach out to some of the parents who couldn't get off work to attend the conferences."

"My mama was one of those parents. She used to leave one job to head to the next before coming home in the wee hours of the morning to do it all again a few hours later."

"Mama Sharon is the hardest working woman I know. She's the reason that I don't judge those parents that can't make it. The other teachers are forever judging them for missing the conferences, and I just know what it's like to have to work hard and be a parent too."

"You have to give your mother credit too. She worked just as hard to raise you," Ericka mentioned my mother.

"She did. Except, she wasn't a single mother. More than half of the parents that I have to email are single mothers. My mom had my stepfather to help raise me. Sharon had her faith to help raise you and your brothers."

Ericka wiped away a tear. "I miss her everyday. It's been so hard having everything I have and not having her here to witness it."

Mama Sharon died a few years ago. Neither of us has truly recovered from losing her. Sharon was like a second mother to me. I spent the majority of my weekends at their house. Every home cooked meal I had was at Mama Sharon's home. My mother was a free spirit who never cared to learn how to cook. My stepfather was the one who taught me how to cook and cooked meals for us. I loved my mom dearly, and appreciated how much she taught me how to be free, she just wasn't the Mama Sharon type of mom.

I closed my laptop and moved closer to Ericka. "I know, babe. I miss her everyday too. Just know she's looking down at you and she's proud of the wife and mother you are today."

Ericka dabbed the tears from her eyes and sniffled. "She'd be cussing me out for leaving Mitch alone with Kalani," we both laughed because Mama Sharon loved her some Mitch.

"She would be cussing you out. Mitch was her baby, and you know she always took his side in everything." You couldn't tell Mama Sharon that Mitch wasn't her son. The day he and Ericka got married was the best day of her life. "I have something that will make you feel better."

"What's that?" she sniffled and continued to struggle to pack her bag. "Girl, I'm going to be pissed if they charge me a damn fee."

"Enough about the fee. Remember my student's father that we met the other night?"

"Uh huh."

"Well, he asked me out on a date."

Ericka's head popped up and she forgot all about her suitcase struggles. "Madison! Are you freaking kidding me?"

"It's not really a date. He just wants to show me around Brookwood, and I agreed."

I agreed to go out with Parker because I guess I was curious about him. From what I knew he was a single father to an amazing kid and he worked a lot – per Angel's words. Even with Angel mentioning how much he worked, he still spoke so highly of his father. I was curious how a man like that ended up becoming a single father. Per Angel, his mother was getting remarried and he was happy for her. After meeting Parker, I wondered how his feelings were about his ex-wife's impending wedding.

"Maddie, it's a damn date. No man offers to show anyone around without it being a date. He wants to feel you out. What did you say?"

"I accepted his invitation. You said that I need to get out there and do something."

"You absolutely need to. It's not like your dating profile is going to pull anybody in."

"Can you stop coming for my dating profile? I worked hard as hell on that profile and I've gotten a few hits."

"Maybe you need to work a little bit harder on it. Anyway, when is this date? Do I need to stay a bit longer to make sure that everything goes smoothly?"

I rolled my eyes at her. "You need to get your butt on that plane back home to my godbaby and your husband."

"You're never any fun. I wanted to

stick around and hear all the juicy details. We all know that you'll call me three days later."

"I promise I will call you before and after the date. He didn't even ask me for my number, so I think he was just making small talk," I shrugged.

As much as I wanted to believe that he was serious, he was probably just making small talk and wasn't serious about us going out. I wasn't hurt by it because it felt nice to flirt again. It had been a while since I had even opened myself up to flirting with a man again. After Joshua called off our wedding I didn't think I would ever love again. Howe could I love again? This man was my everything and he decided that he didn't want to marry me. What hurt the most was the fact that he never gave me a reason why. I continued to live day in and day out wondering what *I* did wrong to deserve this? It scared me to give my heart to another man. As much as I believed in love and wanted to experience it again, there was some type of fear involved with it too. What if I gave my heart to another man and he decided that he didn't want this anymore? I don't think I could handle something like that again.

"Perfect. I want all the juicy details too," she smirked when she successfully closed her suitcase.

"Details of what? Brookwood? I'll be sure to describe every landmark he brings me to," I sarcastically replied and walked out the room.

Ericka followed behind me. "I want the juicy details of the sexual attraction that's going to be brewing the entire time he's showing you these boring landmarks."

I grabbed some glasses and a bottle of wine for us to enjoy on her last night here. Having Ericka here was a small reminder of being back home. I loved having her here and it did make me miss home a little bit. I was so used to her getting in her car and driving back to Jersey, and now she was going to be boarding a plane to head back home. This little visit was needed, and I didn't realize just how much I needed it.

"I can't believe your trip is over already," I sighed and poured wine into both of our glasses.

Ericka had thrown my throw over her legs and got comfortable on the couch. I handed her a glass of wine and sat down next to her. "Me too. I wish I could extend my trip."

"You can always just move here," I joked.

"Girl, no. Mitch would think I was going through a midlife crisis or something," she joked. "It wouldn't be so bad since his layoff. That's why he stressed me getting away for a little bit."

Mitch worked as a banker, and the firm he worked for did massive layoffs. Unfortunately, Mitch was one of those people who ended up being laid off. When it happened, Ericka called me crying. My first instinct was to hop on a plane and be there for my friend. Before I could even book my flight, she stopped and told me to stay. I had to realize that she was a wife and all she wanted to do was vent. Ericka was the type that cried before picking up her pants and handling her business.

"How has it been? Any luck with the job search?"

Ericka took a sip of her wine and sighed. "Every interview goes well until it comes time for a call back. He either never hears back from them or they're paying way too low. He's trying, Madison. He really is and I feel so bad."

"I know it's stressful for you with it being a single income household."

"His unemployment ended a month ago. We're living off my salary and our savings. Mitch hates this and I hate this for him."

"He's a provider, so I know it can't be

easy with him sitting back and watching you work."

"It's not. Things around the house are tense because of it. I know Mitch loves me, and I love him too," she paused, "but I'm tired of arguing over small things. I know it's because he feels like less of a man because he's unemployed right now. I keep telling him that this isn't forever, and we're going to get through this."

"You are. This is one of the storms that the pastor spoke about at y'all wedding. You will come out if it, it will get better and then the sun will shine," I touched her hand while she wiped away her tears.

"I pray it does."

Ericka was strong because she had watched Mama Sharon be strong. Even before she met her husband she was determined. Ericka worked for the city and was a therapist for at risk foster children. These cases she had were so mentally draining and heart wrenching for me. How she got up everyday and did her job was beyond me. Ericka was a damn superhero in my eyes. When we were roommates, I watched her come home and sob because of a case she was working. She would never tell me about the cases, but from the bottles of wine she consumed I knew that they were heavy. Every so often one of her cases made it to the news and she'd nod to let me know it was one of hers. Her career meant the world to her, even though she wasn't compensated well enough, she showed up every day for those children.

"It will. God doesn't give us more than we can handle."

"I love you."

"Love you more," I moved over and hugged her. "More than you know."

* * *

I spoke too soon with Angel not having friends. Julian Monroe was a new student in my class, and both he and Angel clicked. So, I was stuck eating a kale salad alone without my favorite Uno player. I was happy for Angel though. When we had lunch together he always talked about how he wished he had friends he could eat lunch with. Julian came into our class at a perfect time. Julian's mother was one of the moms that couldn't make it to the parent-teacher conference. She was a single mother doing it on her own, and his father was in the military.

As I shoved a fork full of kale into my mouth, my phone started to ring. This was around the time that my mother or Ericka would call to catch up. "Hello?" My voice was muffled because I was trying to quickly choke down the kale.

"Madison Shaw?" I immediately recognized Parker's voice. From the tone of his voice he didn't recognize my muffled one. "Hello?"

"Hey," I gulped down the rest of the

salad. "It's Madison Shaw. May I ask who is speaking?" I already knew, just didn't want to seem like I was waiting on his call.

"It's Parker Woods," he replied.

"Hey Parker. You'll never guess what Angel is doing today?" I was excited to tell him that Angel made a friend.

"What's that?"

"He made a friend and he's having lunch with him today!" I squealed.

"That's my Pop... I knew he would make a friend. He just needed to find the right one," I could hear the pride in Parker's voice through the phone.

"Exactly."

The line grew quiet.

"I told you that I wanted to show you around Brookwood. Did you think I wasn't a man of my word?"

"Not at all. Just wondering how you got my number?"

"You always add it onto your mail blast that you send each week for the kids," he reminded me and all of a sudden I felt stupid.

"Oh."

Parker chuckled. "Anyway, I wanted to see if you were available this Friday?"

"Hmm," I quickly pulled my planner closer to me and checked for Friday. "I don't have anything planned for after school on Friday. What did you have in mind?"

He chuckled. "You'll see on Friday."

"Wow. Are you really going to do me like that?"

"You ever been surprised before? 'Cause you sure acting like you've never been."

"The last surprise I had changed my entire life, so I'm not too fond of them," I replied, thinking about Joshua.

Joshua calling off our wedding was the biggest surprise I had received in my life. So, I have come to hate anything or anyone who tried to surprise me. I was trying to have a open mind about whatever Parker wanted to do on Friday.

"This is a good surprise."

"Okay," I believed him. Don't know why, but I truly believed him when he said it was a good surprise. "Guess I'll wait until Friday to see what the surprise is about."

"Good girl."

I giggled. "I have to pick the kids up from lunch. So, I'll see you on Friday."

Parker laughed. "Ms. Shaw, I'll be giving you a call tonight too."

"Oh really?"

"Uh huh. I have to get back to work too. Talk to you later, and let my boy know I'm proud of him."

"I sure will." We ended the call and I finished the rest of my salad before preparing the smart board for our math lesson after lunch.

The butterflies in my stomach fluttered around and made me excited for Friday. Even if it was just a casual outing with a potential friend, I was excited. Since I had lived here I hadn't made any friends and spent most of my time alone. It would be nice to make a friend that could show me around the real Brookwood. Even if the relationship wasn't romantic, I could tell I would enjoy being friends with Parker. The few times we spoke he had me all smiles and giggles. I needed that.

5: Parker Woods

I was like a kid waiting for the first day of school so they could show off their new sneakers. Friday was the day I usually went into work later on or worked from home. Today I took off so I could get my home in order and spend a little extra time with Angel this morning. Luna was picking him up from school and her week started with him. I allowed her to get him a day early since she was going to visit her grandmother in Atlanta on Saturday. Angel loved visiting his great-grandmother so I was cool with missing out on one day with him. When you moved with the right intentions for the kid, there wasn't any room for being petty.

As much as I wanted to spend an extra day with my son, I knew that he also enjoyed the road trips to Atlanta with his mother. Luna tried to visit her grandmother every other month. Since her wedding was approaching, she was going to Atlanta to try her dress on and help her grandmother find a dress of her own. Besides her grandmother, she had a couple cousins who had kids that Angel played with too. Whenever Angel came back from Atlanta he always had a ton to talk about, and I loved hearing about his time with his family. Most of my nieces and nephews lived on the West Coast so he didn't get to see them too often.

"I think Ms. Shaw is mad at me, Dad," Angel said while eating his cereal. "I didn't eat lunch with her twice this week."

I didn't mean to laugh at him. "Pop, I

think it's the complete opposite. She loves having lunch with you, but she also loves seeing you have lunch with new friends too."

He did a sigh of relief. "Okay good. Ms. Shaw is my favorite teacher and I can't handle her being upset with me."

"I can promise you that you're good. I'm going to see her later today so I can ask her if you want."

"Another conference?" he asked while scooping more cereal into his mouth. "I thought those were over."

"No conference. You know how Ms. Shaw is new to town?"

"Uh huh."

"I'm going to show her around Brookwood."

Angel nodded his head while he chewed his cereal. "Do you like her, Daddy?"

I choked on my coffee. Angel was very blunt with his questions and I should have been more prepared for that. "Yes, she's a great teacher to you. You like her too, right?"

"No like a boyfriend and girlfriend," he specified.

"Um, I don't know. I'm just taking her out as a friend... not a boyfriend."

"That's what Mama said about Dexter. Now she's marrying him." I don't know how or why I continued to forget that my son was not only ten, but he was his father's child. Angel didn't beat around the bush when it came to his questions and the answers he received. We had to tell him that Santa Clause wasn't real because he had figured out that it was Luna who was wearing boots and stomping on flour to make it seem like it was Santa.

"Friendships sometimes evolve into something more. Mom and Dexter were probably really good friends and that turned into love. Now he's going to be her husband."

Angel looked like he didn't give a damn about what I was chatting about. Angel and Dexter's relationship was a good one. It was one I would want my kid to have with their stepparent. "What if Ms. Shaw becomes your wife? Will you get married to her like mom is with Dexter?"

"I don't plan on getting married again, so you don't have to worry about that, Pop."

"I want you to be happy just like how Mama is."

I smiled. "I'm very happy. You're all I need right now, Pop," I touched his cheek. "Now, finish this cereal so I can drop you to school."

"Okay."

Angel kissed me on the cheek while he ran into school. I waved at a blushing Ms. Shaw while she greeted my son. I had enough time to run errands and finally unpack from my work trip. I was a person who kept everything clean and tidy. If my space wasn't clean then I couldn't successfully operate and felt like my day was going to go to shit. I planned to straighten up my place, unpack and go through the pile of mail that had been accumulating on my coffee table and desk.

Tracy's number popped across my car's screen. "What's up, Trace?"

"I saw your email that you're not coming in today. You good?"

"Yeah, I'm straight. I just have a couple errands to run since I been out of town and then had Angel this week."

"How's my boy?"

"Good. He asked some hard questions this morning."

"Yeah?"

"I'm taking his teacher out later today. You know to show her around Brookwood and maybe get a bite to eat."

"Uh huh... sure... to show her around. There ain't much to show around," Tracy teased. "His teacher fire like that?"

"She's beautiful, funny and the way she cares about Angel shows me the type of person she is."

"She's a teacher. If she didn't care about her students then we would have a problem."

"Nah, like she really goes above and beyond. She has lunch with him every day and they play Uno together."

"Are those stupid ass kids still bothering him?"

"Yeah. There's not much we can do because they're smart enough to do it when other adults aren't around. The school is keeping an eye on it."

"I wish I could be Angel for a day and beat they ass."

I laughed. "You crazy. But, son, she's different when it comes to Angel. I called her the other day during lunch and she was so excited to tell me that Angel made a friend, and he was having lunch with him."

"You sound like you like this teacher

more than Angel does."

"I don't even know her. If we had to go off looks alone then hell yeah. She's definitely the type of woman that I would date."

"She ratchet like that other one?"

"Man, let me live. Why do you keep bringing shorty up?"

"Cause you brought her to my barbecue and everybody couldn't believe their eyes. I'm still getting asked if you're dating that girl."

I dated a stripper a year ago. Did I know she was a stripper when we met – no. She told me that she works nights and usually had her mornings off. I didn't want to assume anything, and damn sure wasn't going to assume that she was a stripper. I didn't have a problem with her stripping if that's what she wanted to do with her life. The problem was the way she acted when she got drunk. She acted like Tracy's barbecue was a damn private room at the strip club. The way she was shaking ass, grinding and gyrating on me had me uncomfortable because there were kids there. I had to take her home and on the ride out of her neighborhood I deleted her number. If we out and having fun I don't mind ratchet behavior. It was a time and place for everything and she had crossed the line with me. The minute you make me feel uncomfortable or feel regret then it was time for you to bounce.

"I deleted her number before I fully pulled out of her neighborhood. She reached out a few times and got the hint."

"Now you've moved onto dating school teachers."

"Not a date."

"It sounds like one."

"She's new to Brookwood and doesn't have any friends. I want to show her around our city, so she can feel comfortable."

"How do you know she's not already

comfortable."

"I don't know. Maybe I want to make her more comfortable. It's a nice gesture, why you making me sound like a creep?"

"I know you and you don't go out your way to show people around Brookwood. Hell, you're always hollering about all the newcomers when there's traffic."

I smirked because it was true. "People change."

"They do." Tracy laughed. "Since this is a friendly date, how about me and Mari have dinner with you guys? She needs new friends and we need a break from wedding planning."

"Sounds like a good idea. I'll text you the restaurant when I settle on one."

"Take her to *Trè*," he suggested.

"I haven't eaten there yet so yeah we can do that."

"You don't know what you missing. Food good as shit, and the owners are a black couple that's new to the area."

"Then you already know that's where we going."

"Cool. Let me get back to work and tell Mari. You know how much they hate being told things last minute."

"For real."

We ended the call and I headed toward Target to grab a couple things I needed to replenish. If it was one thing I missed about being married it was when Luna would pick up everything I needed. I never had to worry about running out of deodorant because she had already stockpiled a bunch so I never had to run out. It took a while before I remembered that I was responsible for getting the toiletries and household items that I needed. Luna was always good at doing the house things, even with her having her own career. These days I spent ten minutes in the dish soap aisle trying to figure out which soap was better for grease.

I pushed the cart out of Target and

called my mother. Whenever I had down time I would always give her a call to catch up. "Hey Parker! I was just thinking about you this morning."

"Were you? What were you thinking about? How I'm your favorite child?" I shared a laugh with my mother.

"Yes I was. I'll deny it if you tell anybody else."

"Your secret is safe with me." I loaded up my trunk with the bags. "How are you and Pops doing, Mama?"

"We're great. Your father is off playing golf with his buddies. I'm baking a cake for the country club competition."

The minute the last child moved out my parents sold their house, which was worth a shit ton more, and bought a small single-story home in a gated community that had a country club. My mother's biggest fear was falling down the steps and breaking her hips. Our childhood home had three stories and as much as it was a fear of hers, it was a fear of mine too. Plus, that house was too much maintenance for just the two of them.

"I hope you're making that honey suckle cake. If so, those ladies don't even have a chance." My mother laughed. Her laughter was enough to brighten your day. My father always said it was contagious and the older I became the more I realized just how true it was.

"I'll let them think their lemon bars are doing something. You know I'll smoke those girls anyway."

My mother was the most competitive person I knew. She ran track when she was in high school and won every completion. She could have went further in track if her father didn't pass away her senior year in high school. Because he passed and she was the oldest, she stepped in place to help care for her siblings along with her mother.

"Don't hurt them too bad."

"How is everything with you, Parker?"

"Nothing much, Mama. Just working and trying to keep up with Angel."

"Oh my sweet baby. I miss him so much... when are you bringing him home to visit us?"

"It's been a while, huh?"

"Since your father's sixty-fifth birthday. We miss having you guys around," she paused. "How's Luna been?"

"She's doing good. I think she's in wedding planning mode with Dexter."

"How wonderful. I'm so happy that she's getting to plan her wedding the way that she wants. I feel so bad for the way I made her have lavender flowers and she hates the color."

I couldn't hold my laughter in because she was so serious. My mother's biggest regret has been the floral arrangements that she guilted Luna into. "Mama, I don't think she's even thinking about that anymore."

"Who knows? She might have flashbacks the way I hollered at her in the floral shop that day."

"Mama, you got me out here laughing like a fool."

She chuckled. "I'm serious, Parker. Luna is a strong woman, but she ran out that floral shop in tears. I still think about it to this day."

"Why is this the first time I'm hearing this story?" I wiped the tears that fell out the corner of my eyes.

Luna always talked about the horrors of planning our wedding and she never mentioned this. It was probably best that she didn't because I would have laughed about it in her face. "Who knows. I received our wedding invitation in the mail and sent her a selfie of me holding it."

Just because me and Luna were divorced didn't mean that she didn't still reach out to my parents. They received a Christmas card every year and she always reached out on their birthdays. I did the same when it came to her parents too. There was no bad blood between any of us. They realized that we married too soon and grew apart, and all their focus was on their grandson, Angel.

"Since the wedding is in Brookwood you and Daddy can stay with me. I have the guest room. Don't be quick and try to book a hotel."

"I don't want to take over your space, Parker. Daddy snores and you know I wake up at five every morning."

"I don't care, Mama. If you wake up early then I'll be up with you."

She grew quiet.

"How has dating been going?"

"Mama!"

"What? I'm curious. With Luna getting remarried it makes me wonder when you're going to be ready to meet someone or become serious."

"When it feels right. I'm not rushing

anything right now. You know how that ended last time."

"That's true. Oh, your sister is beeping in on the other line," she said. "Parker, I love you and you need to come visit soon."

"I will, Mama. Talk to you soon."

I ended the call and headed home. My mother worried about me because she knew that I was hurt over the divorce. Just because we both wanted it and knew it was something that needed to be done, didn't mean that it didn't hurt. For a while I was bitter about it and resented Luna. I resented her because I felt like she made it unbearable to be married to her. When I finally decided to go to therapy I learned that she was hurting just as much as I was hurting. While I was resenting her for making our marriage unbearable, she was resenting me for choosing work over her and Angel. We both played our roles in the demise of our marriage and had to move on.

6: Madison Shaw

It took me thirteen minutes and four seconds to make it home after work. I stopped Katherine, the second grade teacher, in her tracks when she tried to hold her usual ten-minute vent about the new school curriculum. We had received noticed two weeks ago and every time she saw my classroom's door open she thought it was an open invitation to come in and vent. Before she could even get a word in today I stopped her in her tracks and told her that I had an important appointment I had to leave for. It wasn't like I attended work looking like I had climbed out of bed. It's just that I wanted to be refreshed and showered before Parker picked me up for our *scheduled tour*. Earlier I had asked if he wanted to meet somewhere or if he wanted to drive together. He said that he wanted to pick me up, so I gave him my address. It wasn't like he was a complete stranger. After all, he did trust me with his son for seven hours a day, so giving him my address wasn't that big of a deal.

"He's going to be here in twenty minutes and I don't know what to do with my hair," I groaned while on FaceTime with Ericka.

She was sitting at her desk, pulling overtime, and I could tell that she was overwhelmed. Ericka was so selfless that even if I asked what was wrong, she would never talk about herself because she knew I was going out tonight with Parker.

"Put some leave in conditioner in and

brush it up in a big bun. I love when you wear your hair in a big fuzz ball."

My hair fell down my back even when it was curly. Whenever I had the time I would straighten it and wear it like that until the next wash day. This week I decided to keep my natural texture, and now I was slowly regretting it. How was I supposed to wear my hair tonight?

"A fuzz ball doesn't sound cute."

"Pull it up into a bun and leave a few pieces loose. It's a cute and simple look without doing too much."

I started raking the leave in conditioner into my hair and pulling it up into a bun. Once I secured the bun I pulled a few pieces to give it that messy cute look that Ericka was referring to. "This does look cute."

"Are you nervous?"

"A little. I feel like I may be looking too deeply into this outing. What if he's just being nice and I'm literally planning our wedding?"

Ericka laughed. "Not planning your wedding. Shit, with how fine that man was I would be planning my own wedding too."

"Girl, you feel me."

"Seriously, Maddie. He asked you out because he's not blind. Just like you saw how fine he was, he was checkin' you out too. You're beautiful, educated and you're a godsend with those children. The perfect woman."

"I may not be the perfect woman for everybody," I rolled my eyes while applying my makeup.

"Joshua was an asshole. Last I heard he was traveling abroad trying to find himself. Not saying there's anything wrong with that, but did you really want to marry a man who couldn't find himself? What if you got married and he decided to pull this *eat, pray love* bullshit on you... imagine how that would have been."

"Yeah. That would have been tragic."

"You see. Things happen for a reason. Go out tonight and enjoy yourself without thinking anything needs to come from it. What if a good friendship comes from going out tonight... stop overthinking and enjoy you—"

She was cut off when my doorbell sounded. "He's here," I whispered, as I lined my lips quickly.

Since I moved to Brookwood I did a simple makeup routine that had me out the door in under ten minutes. Back home, I used to take thirty minutes just to apply my makeup. Here, with this little natural beat that I did, men looked my way so it must have been good.

"Go and enjoy yourself. I love you and call me tomorrow and fill me in. Unless he's laying next to you, then call me Sunday."

"Girl, you are too much. Love you," I ended the call with Ericka, and then I went to check myself over in the mirror.

Since Parker told me the vibe tonight was casual, I wore a pair of high rise wide legged jeans that hugged my curves perfectly. To se the outfit off, I wore a distressed Golden Girls crop top and the pair of Tom Ford heels my mother bought me for my bridal shower. They were golden with a lock on the ankle, and if I knew they hurt as much as they did, I would have told her to save the money. I had to admit though, the outfit was cute and the heels pulled it all together.

"Hey Parker!" I greeted when I opened the door. Like Ericka said, I needed to just be myself and stop thinking this was ever going to lead to anything.

"H.. Hey Ms. Shaw," he stammered while he looked me over. The sexual attraction between us was evident. Neither of us could pretend like it didn't exist.

The two times I met Parker he wasn't dressed down much. Well, the first time I didn't notice what he had on because I was leaned over the booth. When he rushed into my office he was dressed in a suit. Tonight, he wore a pair of tan cargoes with Jordan's and had a hoodie on. He wore a hat over his waves and he even tossed in a pair of grills.

"Didn't I tell you about that?"

"Damn, I can't help it when you're looking this good," he smirked. "I know I told you casual. Just didn't think you were going to outdo yourself like this."

"Come in. I just need to choose my perfume tonight and then we can go. I don't know what kind of tour we're doing when the sun is about to set."

"C'mon you not playing fair."

"How you figure?"

"Looking like that and putting on perfume... not fair, Ms. Shaw."

I blushed. "I never play fair."

"Man, that line was so corny."

We broke out in laughter because the thought had popped in my head. I just didn't think he would be bold enough to say it to me. "Where are we going tonight?"

He rubbed his hands together and stood in my living room. "My friends are meeting us at this new restaurant in town. I figured since our days ran long we can do the tour another day."

"Your friends? I'm down for meeting new people...right now the only new people I've met are the people in the book I just started."

"That's good. My best friend is bringing his fiancée, and you both should hit it off well."

I quickly went into my room to rub some Egyptian oil on the nape of my neck and layered it with my favorite Arabic perfume that I ordered off Amazon. "I'm excited. Besides when my best friend came, I haven't been out at all."

"Good thing I asked you on a date."

I poked my head out my bedroom. "A date? What happened to you being the welcome committee?"

Parker grinned. "I'm still the welcome committee. You can't open the door looking like that and expect me to not label this a date."

My heart fluttered at the sound of him calling this a date. "I'm ready for a drink and some appetizers."

"Before meeting up with my friends I want to take you to grab a quick drink at my favorite bar."

"Sounds good," I grabbed my purse and turned out the lights in my bedroom. Parker held the door open for me, and I locked up.

He was parked in front of my apartment building. Like the gentleman he was, he opened the door for me. "How was work today?" he asked while getting into the car.

His scent was all over this car and it was intoxicating. A good smelling man was a weakness for me. If only Parker knew how much I was turned on by him. "It was great. The kids got the chance to work on their science projects all day. I can't wait to see their presentations next week."

"You really love this teaching shit, huh?"

I smiled. "Yes. I've always loved children, so getting to spend time with my students every day is a highlight for me."

"You light up whenever you talk about the students. Especially when you talk about my son."

"Angel is such a special child. I enjoy seeing him run into class every day," she continued to sing Angel's praises.

"He really is. Did you get a chance to talk with his mother when she picked him up?"

"His stepfather picked him up. I think his mother had to stay late at work."

"Oh, Dexter."

"Yes, that's his name. He's a good guy. Was super interested in Angel's project," I explained.

Angel told me about his stepfather. I loved how positive the adults surrounding him were. He was able to articulate exactly how he felt about his mother getting married again. I've taught plenty of children that were the product of divorce, and almost all of them hated the fact that their parents weren't together anymore. Angel knew exactly why his parents divorced and knew that they loved him, and his new soon to be stepfather was going to give him extra love.

"Yeah Dex is my guy."

The ride was a comfortable silence. Neither of us rushed to speak or ask questions and it wasn't awkward at all. I took in the unfamiliar scenery as he drove us to the bar. My GPS gave me one way to the school and it was the only way that I took. Besides when me and Ericka went on a hike and to Red Lobster, I didn't really get out too much. At the moment I lived in an apartment and didn't have any real plans to move any time soon. Eventually, I wanted to own my home here in Brookwood. Passing by the beautiful craftsman's style homes with tons of character inspired me. I could see myself in the front yard watering and planting flowers while my future husband was putting steak on the grill for dinner.

"My best friend texted and said they're running a little bit late, so we're good to stop and have a drink before heading over to the restaurant."

"That's cool. I've never been this way before... you managed to make it to Brookwood square quicker than me."

"I bet you're following that GPS. Some of these streets are new to Brookwood, so it's not registered on the GPS yet. Gotta learn to navigate these streets," he teased.

"Listen, I thought I was tough shit when I made it to Publix without needing it," I giggled.

"I'll be your chauffeur any day. What is it that you women call riding shotgun these days?"

"Passenger Princess," I blushed. "Don't write a check your ass can't cash... 'cause, I'll take you up on your offer all the time."

"I don't offer anything that I'm not ready for," he licked his juicy thick lips while backing up into his spot.

Besides a good smelling man, the second sexiest thing was watching a man hold the back of the passenger seat arm rest while backing into a parking spot. Witnessing Parker do it in this moment had me ready to jump his bones.

"Good to know."

Like the gentleman that he was, he walked around the car and opened the door for me. I held onto his hand while I stepped out of his car. Brookwood square really came alive when the sun started to set. During the day you could find the older crowd enjoying the brunch specials and the shops that littered the area. Soon as the sun started to set the crowd changed. Bars put their written signs on the sidewalk, and you noticed women dressed up holding hands with their dates. The vibe was a welcomed change from New York. Everyone was just existing in their own worlds, and I loved it.

"This is one of my favorite bars in the area. I come here quite a few times during the week to have dinner and a quick drink."

"Sounds like you may need a home cooked meal."

"It's been a while since I've had one of those," he winked while holding the door and using his hand to guide me into the bar.

The upscale bar was just my taste. I half expected him to bring me to a pub to grab a drink. The contemporary decor and the R&B music made the environment so much more chilled. Even if he took me here as the date I wouldn't have minded because it such a vibe here.

"Hey Parker, come I have a spot right here for you," the tatted bartender waved us over.

Parker put his hand on the small of my back and guided me over toward the bar. "What's up, Guy?"

"Ain't shit up but the sky, Park... sit down and let me make you and your beautiful friend a drink."

Parker smiled because he knew I made him look good. It had been a while since I felt this confident. Ever since Joshua broke my heart I had retreated back into a shell. It was already bad that I had to call friends and family and tell them the wedding was off, what made it worse was the fifteen pounds I had gained from eating my emotions. With the way that Parker kept stealing glances I knew I looked good, and that was his way of telling me without words.

"This is my special friend, Madison Shaw. She's a teacher at Brookwood elementary. Madison, this is Guy Ortiz... he owns the bar."

"Nice to meet you. This bar is amazing... you may have a new customer stopping by," I shook his hand.

"Brookwood elementary. My son is in fifth grade there... I hear an accent... don't tell me we got another New Yorker around town."

"Brooklyn all day," he held his hand out and dapped me up.

"Hell yeah... BK all day. It's nice to have another New Yorker around here." Guy smiled and started making drinks. "Any allergies that I need to know about?"

"Nope. I'm good with anything that you make."

"What am I chopped liver? I'm not from New York, but Jersey is close enough."

Me and Guy both looked at Parker and busted out laughing. "I love you, bro'… it's a bond that Brooklynites share that nobody else does. Your drinks will be right up," he tapped the bar and then went to make our drinks.

"You throwing me under the bus already?" Parker chuckled and turned to look at me.

"It's the Brooklyn way," I teased.

Guy came back over and put two ombré colored drinks in front of us. "Our coconut sunset cocktail. It's something I'm working on adding to the menu. I put in an order for a basket of truffled fries too."

"Good looks, Guy." Parker dapped hands with Guy before he went to serve some other patrons down the bar.

"Always, Fam."

"How long have you've known Guy?"

"Going on two years now. *Bebar* is the only Spanish bar in the square."

"Wow. That's huge. This place is amazing and I see why you're always here. It gives you a calm vibe soon as you walk in."

"After having a stressful day I grab a few drinks and eat whatever's on the menu that night and head home. Angel even comes with me to pick up food on the weeks that I have him."

"I thought you were about to say that you bring him to the bar with you."

"Nah you trying to get me a case." We both broke out into a laughing fit. "Angel's mom would kill me if I brought him to eat at a bar."

"Red Lobster has a bar."

"That's different. It's also a family restaurant too."

"What is his mother like?" I felt the

need to ask. This didn't seem like two people getting to know one another as friends. Parker seemed interested in me, and the feeling was mutual.

"Luna is good peoples. She's smart, beautiful and has a dirty sense of humor. It was the reason I fell for her in college."

"Awe, college sweethearts."

"Yeah. We thought we would end up together forever. Life really be throwing curveballs out here."

"What went wrong? It's hard to imagine that you two are divorced and you still talk about her with such respect. All of my separated or divorced friends hate their ex-husbands."

"We both know what we did to fuck our marriage up. Neither of us played more of a part than the other. I had my shit with me and I wasn't the perfect husband, and she had her shit... she was the perfect wife though. I can honestly sit here and say that she tried more than me at times."

It took a lot for a man to admit his part in a failed marriage. Every time I listened to someone discuss their divorce, or why a relationship ended, they always pointed the finger. It was never the person's fault and nobody wanted to take accountability for their role in the relationship. Parker was sitting in front of me while staring into my eyes telling me that he wasn't the best husband, and that took a lot of maturity and balls.

"It takes a lot to admit your wrongs in a relationship."

"I don't think I'm ready to walk down the aisle again, but I am ready to open my heart again. Being honest is the only way a new relationship can be successful. What good will it do if I sit here lying to you and making my ex-wife seem like the villain? It's clear she's capable of being married because she's about to get remarried." He took a sip of his drink. "I'm the single one out here having meaningless sex with people I don't see a future with."

I decided it was my turn to taste the drink. Like I expected, it was delicious. If I had to describe the drink in one word it would have been paradise. "So, we can admit that you planned on this being more than just a tour around town?"

"Without a doubt. When I saw you poke your head around the booth at Red Lobster I knew I wanted to get to know you."

"At least we're being honest now," I cheesed like a fool. It was something about Parker that made me act like a teenager dating for the first time. He made me want to be flirty, girly while operating in my feminine energy.

"What about you?" he asked while taking a sip of his drink. "With the way you came out tonight, I can only imagine half of Brookwood is knocking on your door."

"Oh please... these people don't pay me any attention."

"Maybe because you're held up in that apartment with that big ass bookcase."

"Don't be talking about my bookcase like that," I teased. "I have an extra room that I plan to make a personal library. Just haven't had the time to do it."

"You stalling."

"I'm not... it's just a sensitive subject for me."

"Take your time." He placed his hand over top of mine and waited patiently for me to spill the beans on my past relationship.

"I was engaged to be married. A month before the wedding my ex-fiancé decided that he didn't want to get married anymore. He called the wedding off, and my heart has been broken ever since."

"Shit. I'm sorry."

"It's not your fault, so you don't have to apologize."

"I'm not apologizing to you." I stared at him in confusion. "It's his loss. I'm sorry that he never got to witness having you as his wife. Then, I want to thank him because he set you free so somebody like me could come scoop you up."

A smile crept onto my face. "You trying to scoop me up, huh?"

He polished off the rest of his drink. "That's to be determined by the both of us."

Guy came over with two more drinks. "Try these next."

"I'm starting to feel like this is a drink tasting." The alcohol was making me extra giggly.

"Damn, she figured me out." Guy laughed. "How was the last drink?"

"Fruity enough to be considered a girl drink, then strong enough for a man to order too. It was the perfect blend between the two. Definitely add it onto your menu."

"Appreciate that."

"You don't wanna hear my opinion?" Parker laughed.

"Not really. She said everything I wanted to hear."

"In that case, go ahead and make us some more of these."

We sat, drank and talked for another hour before Parker realized that we were going to miss our reservation at the restaurant. Being the problem solver he was, he moved us over to a booth in the bar, texted his friends to meet us here and ordered a bunch of appetizers. The vibe remained the same with us talking and laughing with one another.

"I want to know what you want in your next relationship."

That was a good question. A lot of men always asked what a woman wanted in their next man, and never questioned what a woman wanted in her next relationship. As a man, you could be everything a woman wants and bring nothing to a relationship.

"That's a good question." I took a sip of the Grey Goose martini that Guy had made me and put the cup back down. "The most important thing I want is love in a relationship. Growth is important to me too. We can both be in a relationship, but if only one of us is growing then it's not a successful relationship. I want love, hugs, kisses and joy. I feel like my last relationship didn't have any joy. We were two people that claimed to love one another, but in the end if there was any real love or joy we would have made it down the aisle."

"Hmm."

"What do you want in your next relationship?"

"You."

I looked away because this man knew all the right things to say to me. "Stop playing with me and answer the question."

He licked his lips and stared at me.

"Something real. I want to know that no matter what we'll get through things together. I want a relationship where we're open and honest. No matter how hard shit is to admit, we're honest with each other. I felt that was one thing that was lacking in my marriage. We weren't honest with each other and I feel like if we were more upfront and honest about shit then our marriage may have lasted."

I could tell his past marriage was a sensitive subject for him. You could tell from the pain in his eyes that he wished he did things differently. As if it was his biggest regret that he's had. "I like that."

"Is that something that you think that you can do?"

"I can."

He reached across the table and rubbed my hand. "I belie—"

"Sorry we're late, bro'. Somebody couldn't decide on which type of casual she wanted to rock tonight."

I looked up and a tall brown skinned man that resembled Flex from the old sitcoms One on One stood next to a light skinned girl with beautiful curly hair. "It's all good. I know how it is when Mari has to pick an outfit out for an event," Parker joked.

"Fuck you, Parker." Mari giggled. "Hey girl, I'm Mari," she introduced herself and slid into the booth.

Parker had gotten up and joined me on my side so they could sit on the other side. "I ordered some food that should be coming out soon. Guy should be over here with more drinks... he saw you come in?" Parker asked.

"Yeah, he saw us. Nice to meet you Madison... I'm Tracy," he introduced himself to me.

"Nice to meet the both of you," I smiled.

Tracy took his jacket off and clapped his hands together. "I see me and Mari are going to have to catch up," he pointed to the empty glasses that were on the table.

"Pretty much. You came all late and shit." Parker waved Guy over.

"Double date... I like it," he dapped Tracy. "I'm going to bring out a few drinks so that you two can catch up."

I usually hated double dates when I was with Joshua. He would text and let me know we were having dinner with his friends and their wives. I always hated it because it was so boring. The women never talked or seemed interested enough to talk to. Joshua always pretended instead of being his regular self, and I found myself overindulging in drinks just to entertain me. This double date was way different that what I was used to. We were all talking and kicking it, and I almost didn't want the night to end.

"These drinks are needed. We just received the invoice for the florist and we're both going to need to pull long hours at work," Mari laughed.

"A florist? Girl, you don't need a florist... you can literally make your own floral arrangements."

Mari was all ears when I mentioned doing it herself. "Um, I'm liking her already. A girl who likes to save coins is a girl I can be friends with."

I giggled. "My cousin got married last year and we put together her entire floral arrangement. She was quoted at least seven grand, and we did it for two thousand dollars, and that was because she wanted these rare roses that had to be flown in." I quickly pulled my phone out and looked at wholesale floral depots. "There's a wholesale floral depot in Charlotte. I don't mind going with you one weekend."

"Yes, I would love that. I've been planning this wedding with the help of Tracy. All my girlfriends have their own thing going on."

I didn't want to reveal that I had been planning my own wedding on my own. It was the reason I knew so many cheap loop holes when it came to planning a dream wedding. "We'll exchange numbers before the night is over."

"Exactly. 'Cause I'm going to have to show you around Brookwood... 'cause it's clear that Parker failed."

Parker eased his arm around my waist. "I wouldn't say I failed."

"He's real slick," I smiled and accepted the drinks that Guy put down onto the table.

We all sat and talked like old friends. Everything felt so natural. From Tracy's corny jokes to Mari trying to get everybody to link for karaoke next weekend. This was so needed for my soul. For once I didn't feel like a stranger in a new city. The way they have embraced me made me feel like this move was worth it.

Tracy had one drink and continued to

have water when he saw how much Mari was drinking. When she started slurring and knocking glasses down he decided to call it quits for the night. After all the drinks I had consumed I was surprised that I was able to stand straight. In between each drink I made sure I sipped water and ate the garlic bread on the table to soak up the liquor. Even with how much water and bread I had been consuming, me and Parker both knew that we shouldn't get behind the wheel. Guy promised Parker that his car was safe, and I ordered us an Uber back to my place.

7: Parker Woods

Madison stared into my eyes as we rode the elevator up to her floor. We consumed too much alcohol and some how we weren't sloppy drunk or belligerent. I reached out and touched her cheek. She looked to the left and avoided eye contact with me. I wanted to know what was going on in that head of hers. She was so beautiful to me, and I just wanted to know everything about her. The elevator stopped at her floor and she grabbed my hand, pulling me behind her. On the Uber ride over here she held my hand while I watched her stare out the window.

If you would have told me that our date would have ended with me going back to her place, I would have laughed. The most I thought would come out of tonight was drinks and dinner. Madison carried herself like the type of woman that didn't invite men back to her place. While I followed behind her as she held my hand, I watched her unlock the door to her place. Even though she was moved in, you could tell from the few moving boxes that everything was completely unpacked.

"We've been drinking all night, so do you want water?"

"Please," I leaned on the wall and watched as she put ice cubes into the glasses and filled them with water. "Your house smells like a home... it's weird. Some places have a smell that just reminds you of home."

"Thank you," she handed me the glass. "What does your home smell like?"

"Not a home."

"Stop. I'm sure it smells like home... Angel thinks your apartment is the best," she pulled me over toward the couch. I had to be honest, I liked the way she kept pulling me where she wanted me to be.

"For real?"

"Yeah. He says that your house is the man bat cave," I chuckled. Angel always called my apartment the bat cave.

I didn't spend as much time making my apartment into a home. Don't get me wrong, it was comfortable... it just wasn't Madison's place. Even with the few packing boxes, you could tell she knew how to make a place her own.

"He's funny."

Pretty feet was a weakness for me. If a woman had pretty feet they could walk all over me. Madison had pretty white toes that had the imprint from the heels she had been wearing all night. I sat my glass on the coaster and pulled her feet into my lap. She was impressed and allowed me to gently rub her feet while staring into her eyes.

"I could get used to this," she admitted.

"Me too."

"Rubbing feet?"

"Yeah. Especially after a long day of work. Chilling while watching our favorite shows and catching up on each other's day."

"It sounds like a dream."

"A dream that could very well be our reality one day."

"Yes. One day."

"One day soon."

"Parker," she blushed. "How many other women in Brookwood are you telling this to? I know you're dating other women."

"I wouldn't even call what I'm doing

dating. Hooking up… yeah. Dating… nah," I admitted.

It was true. I've gone on a few dates after my divorce and couldn't connect with any of them. Maybe it was because I was still healing from the divorce, or maybe because none of the women were worth trying to connect with. After going on dates and wasting money, I started to be honest with myself. All I was really looking for was sex. It was what I wanted, not a relationship. Though a relationship was what I craved, I couldn't see myself settling down with any of those women. Angel was an important factor for me, and I couldn't see myself introducing him to any of them.

Madison on the other hand was different. Since the first time I laid eyes on her, I wanted to know more. What made her move to a small city like Brookwood? She was so different from the women in this town that I couldn't stop thinking about her. Especially after the conference we had.

Seeing a woman care for my son the way she did, did something to me. Angel spoke so highly of her that I would be a fool not to at least ask her out and see if the chemistry I was feeling was all in my head.

"Our date was great, and I really enjoyed myself. That doesn't mean I'm ready to turn in my keys and move in with you," she paused. "How do you know this is what you want after one date?"

It was a valid question. A man could say anything when he's had more than a few drinks. How did she know that it wasn't the drinks talking for me? "I don't know what the future holds for us. All I know is that I want to continue to get to know you... I don't want tonight to be the end of us hanging out."

"Awe, are you worried I'm going to ghost you?" she joked with me.

"Shit, maybe. From the way you talk about your past with your ex, I would assume you would try to protect your heart."

"Are you someone I should be protecting my heart from?"

I leaned forward while still rubbing her feet. "Never. What are your fears with jumping into something like this?"

"Getting hurt again. I think that's any woman's fear when starting a new relationship," she paused and then looked at me. "When I'm in a relationship I'm guilty of loving hard. Probably a little bit too hard. I know I'm worthy of being loved the same exact way. It's a fear of mine to love a man as hard as I loved my ex-fiancé, and he doesn't feel the same about me."

"That's a legitimate fear."

She gently took her foot and sat on it, while looking at me. "What are your fears on jumping into another relationship?"

"Pushing the right person away."

"Why is that a fear of yours?"

I sighed. "Because I know I did that to my ex-wife. I pushed her away when she was trying. We both have our faults and did wrong in our marriage. It was me who pushed her away because I was so focused on my work and trying to climb the corporate ladder."

"Then don't make the same mistake, Parker. Even if your next relationship isn't with me, make sure you don't repeat the same things that ended your marriage. A failed marriage is a learning tool, so use it."

It was crazy how I looked at Luna and Dexter's relationship. Dexter was a doctor and owned his own practice here in Brookwood. He was in demand, and on any given day I passed his practice, you could see the parking lot packed with patients. Despite being one of the best Black doctors in Brookwood, he always made time for Luna. She could call him in the middle of a patient, and he'd be coming to her ten minutes later. I always admired the fact that he was family oriented and put his new family first. He was doing something that I could never do when I was married to Luna. As much as I feared a new relationship, I also feared ruining another relationship more. What if I couldn't be everything to that woman? It was a legit fear of mine to not measure up to my next partner's expectation.

"It's easier said than done." It wasn't like the divorce had forced me to step back and fix the things I've done wrong. If anything, it gave me more of an excuse to work more. I didn't have a wife nagging me and on the weeks I didn't have Angel, I didn't have to feel the guilt of not coming home.

I looked at my watch. "You can stay the night if you want."

Madison didn't look like she was ready for me to leave, and I had to be honest – I wasn't ready to leave either. "Can I kiss you?"

"Please," she moaned and I moved closer to her.

Our lips pushed against each other and I held the back of her head while I shoved my tongue into her mouth. "Come here," I pulled away and allowed Madison to straddle me.

I pulled her shirt up over her head and unbuckled her bra. Madison's pretty breast fell from the bra and sat up on her chest perfectly. Taking one nipple into my mouth, I unbuttoned her jeans and touched her pussy. She was ready for this and wanted this badly. Shirtless with her pants unbuckled, I rubbed her pussy a few times before she jumped off top of me.

"I haven't had sex in a while. Parker, I don't want to start something neither of us can finish."

Now it was my turn to take her hand. I stood up, grabbed her hand and guided her to the bedroom. Since she lived alone I didn't need to worry about closing the door. Madison plopped down on the bed and I watched her breast bounce on her chest. I pulled my joggers down and exposed my hardened dick. She drooled at the sight of it and stood to pull her jeans down. Like i imagined, her thick thighs jiggled while she stepped out of the jeans, exposing the satin pink thong that was barely visible.

"If you're worried about me not finishing this, I have all intentions to finish what I start," I walked over and kissed her in the mouth. "I've been day dreaming about what that ass looks like outside of those jeans," I took a handful of her ass and pushed her onto the bed.

Madison was breathless. "Do you have a condom?"

I dug down into my joggers for my wallet and pulled out a condom. Being single you needed to be prepared for whatever. "Right here."

Madison leaned up and watched me glide the condom over my dick. She opened her legs and patted her pussy making me even harder. I loved a woman with a bush, and Madison had exactly that.

She kept hair on her pussy and still had it neatly trimmed. That naked pussy shit was for the birds. I wanted my woman with some hair on her shit, and Madison didn't disappoint.

I leaned over the top of her and sucked on her bottom lip. Madison roped her arms around my neck and stuck her tongue into my mouth. I maneuvered my hips and found my way into her opening. While we continued to swap spit, I pushed myself into her. Madison moaned into my mouth and opened her legs wider. She was so warm and tight that I never wanted to pull out of her. Madison gyrated her hips while I moved slowly. When she looked me in the eyes and did a simple peck on the lips, I think that's when I lost it. Picking her leg up, I held it up over her head and slammed my dick into her. Madison tossed her head back by moaning out and rubbing her pussy while flicking her nipples at the same time. The mini show she was putting on for me was about to make me cum before her, and I was working hard not to. I leaned down and kissed her again before flipping her over and having my way with her.

* * *

"Madison, your phone," I groaned while listening to her phone continue to ring. She was laying on my chest with her thick thigh draped across me. We both were too comfortable and tired to move. "Baby, silence your phone and then come lay back down," I gently nudged her again, and she groaned without moving.

Her phone was on the nightstand closest to me, so I silenced her phone. I closed my eyes and attempted to go back to sleep, and her phone started ringing again. "Answer," she moaned out and got even more comfortable in my arms.

I slid my finger across the screen and

put the phone to my ear. "Yo." My voice was groggy as shit and my eyes remained closed because the sun was peaking through the sheer curtains she had hung up in her room.

"Um, hello? Who is this?" a woman shot each question right after the other. "Hello?" she raised her voice when I took too long to speak.

"Parker. Who is this?"

"Where is Madison? Why are you answering her phone?" If I was in front of her she probably would have been rolling her neck while asking these questions.

I shook Madison again. "Maddie, wake up and take this phone."

She finally lifted her head and took the phone from me. "Hey... no... yes... I will later. Can I go back to sleep? Thanks. Love you too," I listened to her one-sided conversation.

She handed me the phone back to put

on the nightstand. "She was ready to fight me behind answering your phone."

"That's my best friend, Ericka. She was with me the night I saw you and Angel at Red Lobster," she mumbled and laid back down on me.

Madison's love language was touch. All night she had to be on or near me while we slept. Not that I minded because I loved affection. The way she took over my body was like she was trying to tell me it was hers.

"Hmm."

"Why you say hmm?" her head popped back up while she looked me in the eyes. Even with her hair matted to one side of her head, a missing eyelash and yesterday's makeup smeared on her face she was still the most beautiful woman in the world.

"Was she hard on you?"

"Nah. She was doing what a concerned friend would do… ask questions."

"It was too much of me to ask you to

answer my phone." Madison was a overthinker and she was the type to apologize for things that weren't even her fault. "Yeah, that was too much," she pulled the covers and climbed out of bed with my shirt on.

I leaned up. "No it wasn't. You were tired and I was tired of hearing your phone ring."

Madison paced back and forth in front of the bed. Watching her ass jiggle as she walked back and forth turned me on. I pulled the covers back exposing my dick. She was so busy in her head that it took a minute for her to notice I was stroking my dick and watching her.

"You ready to stop pacing and put some energy into riding?"

With a sly smile on her face, she pulled my shirt off and curled into the bed for round unknown. I stopped counting after our forth go round.

8: Madison Shaw

The last time I had sex was with Joshua a week before my move to Brookwood. He was coming over to pick up photo books that his mother had lent us for the wedding. We were supposed to give the books to the photographers so they could do a cute slide show that would display at the reception. Since the wedding wasn't happening anymore I wanted to make sure that he received these books. The way his mother acted like these were her prized possessions, I wanted to make sure he held these books in his hands. He had texted and told me that I could mail them to his mother, and I refused. These were all their family memories and I wouldn't be able to forgive myself if something happened while they were in transit.

Before he came over I promised myself that I wouldn't get emotional or talk about our relationship. This visit was for one thing and one thing only – the photo albums. Nerves kicked in and I had three glasses of wine before he even rang the bell. When he came upstairs, he noticed the wine glass and asked if he could join me. My brain told me to give him the books and let him leave my life. It was my heart that wanted this last moment with him. The hopeless romantic in me thought that maybe he might see this breakup as a mistake. It was a stupid thought, but a thought, nonetheless.

The minute he sat down and I poured him a glass of wine I regretted it. I should have shoved the photo albums into his hand

and finished packing. Joshua was all too comfortable sitting and sharing a drink with me after he broke my heart. He spoke about his new place and how he was already having trouble with his neighbor because they had barking dogs. I wanted to scream in his face and tell him that he wouldn't have to move if he didn't throw away our future marriage. As Joshua talked about missing a home cooked meal after work and how he had to figure out a faster route to work from his new place, I realized that this man never cared about me. He loved the idea of having a relationship where a woman put him first.

That was exactly what I did during our entire relationship. I loved Joshua more than he loved me. I put everything that I had into our relationship praying that I would become his wife. Even our wedding planning had all been up to me to do. It was like I was watching Joshua at the kitchen counter we had shared many meals at for the first time. He was so comfortable, carefree and didn't seem like he had been losing any sleep. Meanwhile this makeup covered dark circles that were the size of Pluto, and I hadn't had a decent night of sleep since he called the wedding off. At any given moment I could breakout in tears.

Even after coming to the realization that this nigga wasn't no good, when he kissed and told me that he missed me I folded. Folded like a card table at a Fourth of July barbecue. That was the moment that I should have stood up and sent him on his way. Instead, I allowed him to feed me sweet nothings as he slid up inside of me and I imagined us on our honeymoon that would never be. When he was done, he kissed me on the forehead, got dressed and wished me luck on the move. That was the lowest I had ever felt when it came to being with a man. So, sex wasn't the biggest thing on my agenda when I moved to Brookwood.

Sex with Parker had me grinning from ear to ear this morning while I wrote the task of the day for my students. Our date happened last weekend and I couldn't get it off my mind. Parker had a unexpected work trip out of town, and he was getting back tonight. While he was gone we would text during the day and sit on FaceTime at night. He would sit on the phone and watch me do my skincare routine while cracking jokes. Everything was so easy when it came to us that I wanted someone to pinch me and tell me it was a dream.

The things I begged Joshua to do during our relationship, Parker did without me having to mention it. He sent flowers to my classroom that Monday after our date, and he called me randomly during the day and told me he just wanted to hear my voice. I used to sit and ask Joshua to show me he cared by doing those things and he always had an excuse. It was always something as to why he couldn't do what he should have as my man. With Parker, I didn't have to ask because he was already showing me that he wanted me. I didn't have to beg or drop hints because he knew what he wanted, and he had no problem going after it.

When he left my apartment Sunday afternoon I didn't want him to leave. We spent the entire weekend together and ordered food in. Besides being occupied with sex, we talked and just spent time. I loved being on him and feeling his warmth next to me. Parker made me feel comfortable to be clingy, although I tried not to be. Whenever I moved to give him space he pulled me back over toward him. That was one thing that Joshua had complained about in the past. He said that I was too clingy and it annoyed him. I spent so much of that relationship being someone that I wasn't and I suffered. Back then I didn't feel like I suffered because Joshua was who I wanted to be with. Now that I was on the outside looking in, I knew that I wasn't meant to walk down the aisle to him.

Mari's name popping across my screen brought me from my thoughts. "Hey girly. What's up?"

"Are you in the middle of teaching class or something?" she sounded panicked.

"Nope. Just putting their math work up on the board before they come back from lunch. What's up?"

"Whew. I was worried that I was interrupting your lesson."

"You're fine. I keep my phone on silent anyway."

"Remember you told me about the floral shop in Charlotte?"

"The warehouse... yep."

"Are you free to go this weekend? I was going to suggest doing a girl's trip and staying for the weekend. Get a nice hotel, spa treatments and the whole nine yards."

"Hell yeah. I could use a weekend away to decompress. Shoot me the hotel details so I can book my room."

"Perfect. I just need a break from all this wedding planning. Tracy is great, but he doesn't understand the stress I'm under to plan the perfect wedding."

"There's no such thing as a perfect wedding. No worries, I'm here now and I will help you in any way that I can."

"You're a lifesaver... get back to teaching our future generation and we'll chat soon."

"Talk soon," I smiled and ended the call.

When me and Mari met I liked her right off the back. She was beautiful, smart and had a sense of humor. I could also tell that she had stress on her shoulders when it came to this wedding. Although she joked and laughed over dinner about the wedding, I knew what it was like to plan your own wedding. Tracy seemed more involved than Joshua ever was, so she already had one up on me. Planning my wedding was stressful and fun at the same time. I enjoyed adding my own personal touches and finding new ways to blow my guest's mind, then I stressed about invitations and seating arrangements. My mother wasn't the wedding planning type so it wasn't like I could depend on her. Ericka helped me when she could, but I couldn't expect her to quit her day job just to help me plan a wedding I knew I shouldn't have been planning.

A weekend away in Charlotte sounded like something we both needed. Mari mentioned all her friends lived abroad, so they wouldn't be flying in until the wedding. If she needed a stand in maid of honor until her girls got here, then I was willing to do that for her. It wasn't like I had anything else to do besides teaching and sitting home with a glass of wine. It would be nice to pull out my wedding planner hat and help someone else's dream wedding come true.

"Hey, Ms. Shaw." Angel came into my with his favorite Captain Underpants book tucked under his arm. Angel was always the first kid back after recess.

"Hey honey. How was lunch today?"

"Dexter packed me lunch today and it was quite splendid," he mocked a English accent.

This kid was something special. Every day I looked forward to him walking into my class, and doing something that would make me last. He was so smart and quirky that it made him the most amazing kid ever. The other kids didn't understand that Angel would grow up to be someone important one day. Plus, I wasn't a big fan of the kids that bullied him. Meeting their parents told me everything I needed to know about why they behaved the way that they did.

"Did you also have a spot of tea too?" I continued on with the fake British accent. "I take mine with a splash of milk."

"Gross, Ms. Shaw. Milk in honey is gross," he plopped down at his desk. "My mama makes hers with ginger and lemon. It's so good."

"I bet. Does she add some honey in there too."

"Just a splash," he smirked.

Angel had no idea that me and his father were talking. He didn't even know that we went on a date and I told Parker to keep it that way. We weren't together, or even established what it was that we were doing. Before getting Angel involved, I thought it was best that we continue to get one another and decide what we were doing first. Thankfully, Parker agreed.

I watched Parker climb into his mother's truck and she waved as they pulled away. He was the second to last student to leave. While I stood out front of the school with my purse in one hand and school bag in the other, I watched Lilly's mother pull up in front of the school. Lilly's mother was always late. I could always count on staying a couple minutes behind to wait for her. She worked two jobs and had just filed for divorce, so I cut her slack. It wasn't easy being a mother, and here she was being a single mother.

"Sorry for being late," Jazmine got out the car and jogged around the car. "I didn't take my lunch today so I could get out early, and traffic jammed me up."

Jazmine was bi-racial with thick beautiful blonde tresses that were always frizzy and sitting on top of her head. "It's alright, Jazmine. I know how it is with the traffic."

She smiled. "Go ahead and buckle in, babe," she told Lilly, who skipped along and did what her mother asked. "I really appreciate you for not being rude. Last year I had a teacher call CPS on me because I was always late picking Lilly up."

"You're a mama just trying to do her best. Lilly is a respectful child, and I have no problem staying a couple minutes behind to wait for you."

"Thank you, Ms. Shaw."

"No problem," I winked. Jazmine had to be in her early twenties, so I showed her grace. It wasn't easy doing what she did when you felt like the world was stacked against you. She seemed like she married pretty young and the situation was a complicated one. I knew all about complicated relationships and the douche bags who held them together.

* * *

The day had truly drained me by the time I made it home. Usually I headed straight home after work, but today I stopped to grab a few groceries and restock on my favorite cosmetics at Sephora. By the time I had made it home all I had the energy to make was an order on UberEats. Parker had sent me a text telling me that he was boarding his flight earlier. I knew the first stop he would want to make was to see Angel. He explained to me how much he hated traveling for work. With his company doing a merger, and him being the head of his department it was expected for him to go back and forth. This time he had to stay for a week and he complained every time we spoke. He didn't like the fact that he had to travel for his job, especially when that hadn't always been the case.

While I ran my bath, I started to put away my groceries so all I had to do was relax on the couch and watch 911 on the couch. After the long day I had all I wanted was to get ready for the next day.

Here's the hotel. I booked my room. Mari sent me a text message with the link to the hotel we were going to be staying at.

Perf. Going to book now.

I shut the water off and went to my desk to make my reservation for the hotel. As much as I was down for a girl's weekend away, I needed my own room. As I grew older, I realized that I needed my own room on girl's trips. I was a grown ass woman and needed my own space. Just as I was about to book my room, my food arrived.

"Great. I didn't even get a chance to take my bath," I mumbled and headed toward the door. When I swung the door opened Parker was standing there with a smile on his face. "Parker, what are you doing here?"

I was floored that he was even standing at my door. "You're all I could think about when I was riding from the airport. Before I knew it, I got off the highway and ended up here."

I stepped out the door and wrapped

my arms around his neck. "I really wanted to see you too."

We both kissed while standing in the hallway. Parker gripped my ass while I kissed him on the lips and hugged him tightly. "I just popped up on you and don't even know if you're busy or entertaining."

I stepped back and rolled my eyes. "You know damn well I'm not entertaining nobody," I waved for him to come in. "Mari asked to do a girl's weekend to Charlotte this weekend."

"That's good that you're making friends. Mari is good peoples." For the first time I noticed he held a plastic bag in his hands. "I grabbed some appetizers from the bar."

"Yummy. I ordered food, but I can have that for lunch tomorrow."

Parker walked behind me and put his arms around me. "How was your day?"

I turned around in his arms to face him. "It was long."

"I bet. How was Angel today?"

"Good. He's always good you know that," I messed with his shirt while looking into his eyes. "How was your flight?"

"Long."

"It was not that long," I gently punched him. "Seriously, it means a lot that you came to see me after your flight."

"Of course. I wasn't going to be able to sleep tonight if I didn't come see you. Sit down and let me plate dinner."

"You spend the weekend once and you're already acting like you know where everything is."

"I'm the one who helped put the plates away. Remember you couldn't even reach the top shelf."

"Touché," I giggled.

While Parker plated the food, I went back over to my desk to finish booking my hotel room. When I was done I checked a few emails and then went back into the kitchen. Parker had lit a candle, poured us wine and plated the appetizers.

"It's a little something to show you how much I enjoy your company."

Before I knew it, tears welled in my eyes and started dropping down my face. Parker grew concerned and came around the island. "You good, Maddie?"

I reached up and touched his arms. "Yes, I'm fine... I didn't expect to become so emotional."

"Tell me what's up?"

"It's nothing really," I sniffled. "My ex never did spontaneous things like this for me. I always felt like I had to pull teeth for him to do romantic gestures like this. So, this is different for me."

Parker wrapped his arms around me and kissed me on the neck. "To move forward we have to leave the past behind. He wasn't the man for you, so he let you go so a real man like me could slide in."

I giggled. "Oh really?"

"For real. While I was out of town all I could think about was the weekend we shared. I would lay in bed and replay everything about our weekend over and over again, counting down the days until I could check into my flight."

"Really?"

"Madison, I'm really feeling you. Feeling you so hard that I don't want you to have to guess what we're doing."

I held my breath while he spoke. "What are you saying?"

"I want us to exclusively date. All the cards on the table and be real with one another. No more dating apps and meaningless dates."

I reached up and touched his face. "I think we both deserve that."

After Joshua, I had been so hurt that I hadn't dated anybody. I joined a dating app and had a few stupid conversations that went nowhere, but nothing real. Nothing that made me feel like Parker did.

What he made me feel was real and genuine. There wasn't an uncomfortable feeling whenever we got together. Even when he picked me up for our first date. Things happened so naturally and organically for us that I felt comfortable being me.

"I think so too," he reached down and kissed me on the lips. "Come eat because I know you haven't had nothing since breakfast."

That was another thing. From us talking almost everyday he had learned me. He knew that I didn't eat lunch if I was too busy, or I would skip breakfast if I was running late. It was something so small that meant so much to me, and I wouldn't change it for the world.

"I had a few bites of my tuna salad."

"Yeah, alright. Come sit down," he patted me on the butt and pulled me over toward the counter.

I've always been independent. Even

when I was with Joshua, I was still independent. We split the bills and I still did things for myself. It was very rare that he led when it came to our relationship. I always told myself that I didn't mind having a man that wasn't assertive or dominant. I craved to be submissive to my man and I just couldn't be when it came to Joshua. Did I try? Sure. I tried so many times and it never felt right. It always felt forced to me. With Parker, he wasn't afraid to wear the pants and we hadn't even known each other that long. Being submissive came easy, and I was like putty in his hands. This was something I had always wanted for myself and I never thought it would happen like this or so quickly.

9: Parker Woods

Luna had an emergency dress fitting that she needed to attend, so she asked if I could take Angel on her weekend. I would never give up the chance to spend extra time with my son. Dexter never minded taking over when it came to Angel either, so I knew she had no other choice but to call and ask me. Since I had been back from Houston – again, I hadn't got the chance to spend time with Angel and pick his brain. My son was so smart and I loved having conversations with him. It allowed me the chance to truly get to know my son and see how his brain processed things. Angel was always so open and upfront with his emotions so I never had to play the guessing game when it came to him.

"Knock, knock!" I called out as I let myself into Luna's house. She always kept the door unlocked when she knew I was on my way.

"In the kitchen!" she hollered back, so I followed her voice to the kitchen. Luna was packing stuff into a lunch bag with the phone to her ear. "Alright, baby. I love you and will call you when I get on the road," she spoke to, who I assumed, was Dexter.

"Panic in wedding land?" I sat down at the counter and stole a few grapes from the fruit bowl.

Luna snatched the bowl from me. "Excuse me, this is my lunch today. I've been dieting for months to fit into this dress."

"You're perfect the way you are, and I think Dexter feels the same way," I assured her.

Luna smiled. "Thanks, Parker. I also appreciate you taking Angel this weekend. Something went wrong with my dress and they want me to come try it on."

"You know I got you."

"He's cleaning his room that was supposed to be clean last weekend."

"Easy on my boy."

"No, have your boy be easy on me," she laughed. "What's been new with you? I feel like we haven't seen each other in a while. What is new in your life?"

I didn't have any plans on talking to Luna about Madison. When she asked what's new I figured I should mention that me and Madison were dating. "I've been dating."

"That's good. You're always dating though... it's the taking the dating serious that you need to be focused on."

"I take dating seriously."

"Parker, you can't even say that statement without smirking. When have you ever taken dating seriously?"

"When I was with you."

"That's different. I mean since we've divorced."

I reached across the counter and took a few more grapes. "I've been seeing Ms. Shaw."

Luna stared at me confused. "Angel's teacher?"

"Yeah."

"No. End things with her. If things go wrong I don't need her taking it out on my baby."

"She would never do nothing like that."

"Women are crazy these days. You couldn't date somebody that wasn't involved in our son's school?"

"It's not like I planned on it happening that way."

"How did you meet her? At the conference? Maybe I should have gone instead of you." Whenever Luna was stressed she would pace in the middle of doing something. I guess she and Madison were the same in that way.

"Me and Angel saw her at Red Lobster before the conference. I asked to show her around and it turned into me spending the weekend at her apartment."

"So she's easy? That's why you're all of a sudden dating her."

From the way I looked at Luna I could tell she was regretting her words. "Stop with that shit. We're both grown and decided to indulge in adult activities. Don't act like you didn't hand the panties out to Dexter on the first or second date."

I could tell from the way she avoided eye contact that it was true. Luna was holding her noes up like she was a saint or some shit. She slept with Dexter before either of them knew they would eventually end up here planning a wedding.

"Sorry. That was wrong of me to say,"

she quickly apologized. "Our son's teacher, Parker. There are plenty of good women here in Brookwood, why did it have to be her?"

"Why not her? She's a good person, beautiful, smart and she loves teaching our son."

"That's because it's her career. She literally has to love teaching these kids."

"Me and you both know that just because you're a teacher doesn't mean you enjoy your job." I had a few teachers when I was a kid that hated their jobs. They couldn't stand to teach us kids and did the bare minimum. Whenever a teacher pointed out how they still got paid whether we passed or failed, I knew they hated their career choice.

She heaved a sigh and put the rest of her makeshift lunch into the lunch bag. "Do you plan to talk to Angel about it?"

"Yeah."

"Is it really that serious? I mean, you just met her."

It was crazy to admit how serious I was about Madison. Even though we didn't have that much history with one another, I was excited to make those memories with her. I had dated many women in Brookwood and none of them made me feel the way Madison made me feel. It was something about the way she looked up at me with those beautiful brown eyes. As if God had moved her to Brookwood just for me. Whenever I wasn't with her, I thought about the next time I would be with her.

Spending the weekend with her really put everything into perspective for me. The reason I asked her out was because she was beautiful, and I wanted to get to know her more. Madison was more than just beauty. She was smart, funny and caring – all things that I wanted in my next relationship. She was also patient and could understand my hesitation when it comes to wanting to get into another relationship or marriage.

"It's serious for me. Even if nothing comes out of this relationship, I'll be satisfied knowing that I tried something and it didn't work, but I put myself back out there."

Luna had been wanting me to get out and date with a purpose. When I come to her and tell her that I met somebody, now she was hesitant. "I can't tell you how to live your life. Do I wish she wasn't Angel's teacher? Yes. I just want you to be careful and know what you're getting yourself into."

"Says the one who is weeks away from getting married."

We both laughed. "Dexter was different. I knew he would make a good husband, and he and Angel hit it off right away when they met."

"Yeah," I leaned back in the chair.

"I just want you to be happy, Parker. You know that, right?"

I did know that. When we divorced, we couldn't stand one another. Even in the midst of that, Luna cared. She knew that this was the first time we had ever lived apart. So, despite her hating me in that moment, she still found it in herself to check in with me. Even with us being divorced I knew that she worried about me and if I would ever find a relationship after what we had with each other.

"Yeah, I know. All I need is for you to trust that I wouldn't bring this to you unless I was sure."

"We're always on the same page when it comes to Angel, so I know you wouldn't talk to him unless you were pretty serious."

Just as I was about to respond, Angel came running down the stairs. "Daddy! What are you doing here?" Luna didn't tell him that I was coming to pick him up today.

We loved to keep the element of surprise for as long as we could with him. Eventually he'll get older and consider himself too old for our little surprises. "You're hanging with me this weekend, Pop."

"Seriously?" he looked toward his mother.

"That depends. Is your bedroom cleaned?" Luna held her hand onto her hip and looked down at our son.

"Yes, ma'am. I wiped down the window sills like you asked too."

Luna couldn't keep a straight face and folded. "Awe, Papi... you're the cutest," she pinched his cheeks and kissed him on the cheek. "Behave for your father, and I'll pick you up on Monday."

"Mom, gross... your lip-gloss," he wiped his cheek off and stepped back from his mother. "Let me grab my backpack."

He rushed upstairs. Angel never had to pack anything when he went back and forth. We both made sure to keep two of everything at our homes. I didn't want him to ever feel like he was living out of a suitcase when he came to stay with me.

"You used to love my kisses!" Luna called up the stairs and rolled her eyes. "I'm not prepared for this boy to head off to middle school."

"Me either. Our baby boy is growing up and we need to let him."

We both grew quiet.

"Me and Dexter plan to start trying for a baby after the wedding. He doesn't have kids and I would like a second or third."

"You don't have to explain everything to me, Luna. If you and Dexter want to have kids, then have them. We're not married no more so you shouldn't care how I feel about your decisions."

"Parker, you're like my best friend. I want to know your opinion and what you think about it. Do you think Angel will be fine with it?"

I appreciated how my opinion meant a

lot to Luna, even in her new relationship. As much as I wanted to have an opinion on the matter I couldn't. Dexter deserved for his future wife to be sure in the decisions that they made together. I'd be pissed if my wife went consulting her ex-husband about our plans to start a family. If Luna had another baby, I would be supportive because that would be my son's half-sibling.

"Angel has always wanted siblings and neither of us were ready. Thank God we didn't bring another kid into this world. If you feel this is right then do it. Dexter is a good man, loves you and will support you. Go with your gut on this one, Luna."

She smiled. "Thanks."

When Angel came back with his backpack, we headed out. His first request was that he wanted McDonald's. He knew his mother wouldn't give it to him so he always found a way to butter me up. Madison's name appeared across my phone's screen. Angel was already plugged into his tablet with his headphones on, so he wasn't paying attention.

"What's up, Beautiful?"

"Hey," she cooed.

"I miss you already... how has it been?"

"We went to the floral depot and I was able to haggle good prices for Mari's floral arrangements. What are you up to this weekend?"

"Not being between your legs."

"Parker!" she squealed. "Trust that I would love to have that happen... you have no idea. This hotel is beautiful and the tub... I know we can do a few things in there."

"Damn, I'm going to need you quit while we're both ahead. I can't believe you got me missing you like this."

"I feel the same way. It's like a piece of me is missing now that I'm in Charlotte. Please don't think I'm weird," she joked, still, I could tell that she was serious.

Other than what she told me about her last relationship, I could tell that her man had a problem with intimacy. More than a few times Madison had apologized for being overly flirty or revealing how she felt about me.

"You know I like all this shit, right? How could I find you weird when this is what I want too."

"That makes me feel better."

"What are you about to do?"

"Take a quick nap before we explore the city. Mari wants to show me around since she attended college here."

"Dope. I have Angel this weekend, so go enjoy yourself and make sure to call me when you're back at the hotel."

"Really? Is everything alright with his mother?"

"She had a dress emergency in Atlanta, so she's staying the weekend to handle that." Even though I couldn't see her, from her tone, she lit up when I mentioned Angel.

"Have fun on your boy's weekend. I'll talk to you later on," she assured me, and I smiled.

I ended the call and finally handed the worker my debit card. It never failed that there was a damn line wrapped around this McDonald's. "Dad, why were you talking to Ms. Shaw?"

Dammit.

Whenever Angel was tapped into that tablet he never knew what was going on around him. I thought I would be able to speak freely since he had his headphones on too. "Um, Pop..." I stalled.

Even though I had plans on talking to Angel about Madison, I figured I had the whole weekend to do it. "Do you like Ms. Shaw?"

"I do."

"I like Lilly. She's my girlfriend too... I

walked up to her and told her that she was mine, and she agreed."

I couldn't even be serious and busted out laughing. "You just did it like that, huh?"

"If you like somebody then you should tell them and then make them your girlfriend. It's really that simple." I would love to go back to a time when dating was so easy like Angel explained.

"How would you feel if I made Ms. Shaw my girlfriend?"

"Happy. She's a good person and makes me smile. Remember when I hated going to school last year?"

"Yep. I remember."

"Now I love going to school. Even with Billy and Tyler being bullies to me. It's because of Ms. Shaw. She told me that no matter what I always show up to places with my head held high."

"That's great advice, Pop. I'm glad that

you've been following her advice. She is a good person and I like her a lot."

"You don't like a lot of women. That's the reason why you've been single this long."

"What? Who told you that?"

"I heard Mama talking to Granny about it."

I shook my head. No matter how long we've been divorced she was always going to worry about me. "I've been single because the right woman hasn't come along. Pop, the right woman has to be perfect not only for me, but for you too. We share our life together and we need a good person, not just anybody."

"Like how Mama has Dexter?"

"Just like that. Dexter is a good person to not only you, but he's good to Mama too, right?"

"And you too. Dexter really likes you."

"I think he's a cool dude too." I looked at him in the backseat and smiled. "Ms.

Shaw is pretty great. I see why you enjoy spending time with her."

"She listens to me. My old teacher never listened to me and Ms. Shaw does. She asks for my opinion on things too. I like giving my expert opinion."

"Pop, you too much," I laughed.

"Dad, if you like her then you should show up to her house with flowers. Dexter did that to Mama one time and it made her happy for weeks."

"She's out of town."

"Do like the Hallmark movies and show up with the flowers. Where is she?"

"Charlotte."

"That's only four hours away."

"More like an hour with good traffic," I corrected Mr. GPS himself. "She's on a girl's trip with her friend."

"An hour? Dad, buy flowers and let's drive to her... tell her how you feel." Why was I really considering doing what Angel was suggesting? Driving to Charlotte to surprise Madison and tell her how I really feel.

Angel was way too excited to go on this journey with me. "Fuck it, we're driving to Charlotte," I blurted.

"Hell yeah!" Angel agreed and I turned around to check him. "Sorry, Dad... it slipped," he quickly apologized.

"Let's go home to pack some clothes and then stop at the floral shop before we go," I ran down the plan to him.

"Let's do it." We both dapped each other, and I grabbed our food. Was I really about to drive to Charlotte and tell Madison how I felt?

She already knew that I was serious about her. The next step was to make her my girl, and I had to admit that I was nervous. What if she told me she wasn't ready for that? I knew I was ready for this next step with her because she filled me with joy. The fact that Angel liked the idea without hesitation told me that I was making the right move. My past continued to haunt and scare me too. What if I fucked up this relationship too? I remembered all the shit I did in my marriage that caused us to end up here, and I was worried that I would do it again. Madison deserved to be loved and cared for the way that she cared for others, and I just wanted to do that for her.

Work was always going to be number one for me. I enjoyed my job and I never wanted to be in a relationship where I felt like I had to choose. With Luna, I felt like I had to always choose between being a husband and having a career of my own. Yeah, I knew that's not what Luna meant, but it damn sure felt like it some days. With Madison, she was patient and understood my concerns. The way she looked at me and assured me that I wouldn't make those same mistakes always comforted me. This was something that I was meant to do, and it took my son to convince me of going after what I always knew I wanted.

10: Madison Shaw

"Why in the world do I have three missed calls from you?" I laughed when Ericka finally picked up the phone.

She was so giddy with joy that she couldn't even get her words out. "I didn't want to tell you this because I wasn't sure and Mitch forced me to secrecy."

I was growing concerned. If she hadn't been so giddy I probably would assumed someone was sick. "Ericka; tell me what's going on... I can't take this."

"Mitch got a job in Brookwood!" she squealed.

"What?" I hollered. "H...how did this happen?" I stammered, not believing what she had just told me.

"When I got back from visiting you, I was talking to Mitch about Brookwood. I told him how it had the small town feel, and Black people were doing really well there."

"Look at you speaking nice on Brookwood."

"Despite the Red Lobster, I liked the town."

"We have more than that restaurant here... Parker showed me a few others," I explained to her.

There was more restaurants than just in Brook Square. "Anyway, he went onto Indeed and looked up some possible jobs there. There was a position for an equity analyst, and you know Mitch has some background in that. He applied not thinking anything of it, and they called him for a Zoom interview," she paused.

"They hired him on the spot and even added moving expenses to get us down there."

"Ericka, I'm so happy for you guys.... I told you that this was just something you both were going through. What about your job? You love your job."

"Mitch's salary is really good. Plus, with the cost of living there we can afford to live off his salary for a while. I'll resign and probably try to find some work down there... it's for the best though."

"What's wrong?"

"You know I love my career."

"I do."

"It becomes so draining at times. When I come home I have given so much of my energy to those kids that I barely have any left for my daughter. Maybe this move is what we needed to get our home back on track."

It sounded like there was more to what she was saying, and I knew not to push. If or when she wanted to reveal what was wrong she would. "I'm happy for you. I can't wait to have you here with me... girl date nights are back on."

"I could really use one of those right now," she admitted. "Anyway, now that I told you my good news... what's new with you? I feel like we haven't talked in forever."

"I've been good and having even better sex," I snickered like I was a teenager that just lost her virginity to her boyfriend.

"Better sex? It went from a date to sex... what in the world?"

"He's amazing, Ericka. Parker is the man that I was meant to be with," I admitted out loud for the first time. "He doesn't make me feel like I'm doing too much or smothering him."

"Like Joshua."

"Yes."

"I love that for you. You've always showed too much love to Joshua and he never showed you enough. I'm happy that you have someone that will love your baby voice, 'cause lord knows I can't stand it."

"See, I didn't pull the baby voice out right away. I'm not trying to scare him away so quick."

We both laughed.

"Joshua was an asshole who didn't deserve a light as bright as you. If Parker is showing you that this is what he wants, then go for it. Who says that you have to take things slow. You did that with Joshua and he wasted years of her life in the end. Dive all in and live life how you want to live it."

"You're right."

"Don't feel like you need to be working toward an engagement, Madison. Enjoy having a meaningful relationship with Parker. All that other stuff will come if it's meant to be," she warned me.

I was so used to feeling like I had to be working toward something. In a relationship, I felt that the next step was marriage. Now that I had time to sit back and analyze things, I knew Joshua proposed because I pressured him to. Marriage wasn't in his plans and his actions showed me that before his words did. I was so busy wanting things my way that I turned a blind eye and ignored the red flags. Joshua would have never proposed to me if I wasn't pressuring him to do so.

"You're right." As much as I hated to admit that she was right, Ericka was always right. "When does he start his job here?"

"Next month. We're trying to put the house on the market and scramble. More than likely he'll come down to secure our housing before us."

"Well, when you guys do get settled we're doing a girl's trip to Charlotte."

"Um..C..Charlotte? What's in Charlotte?" her voice was nervous.

"That's where I am right now. Me and my friend Mari drove here to spend the weekend. It's relaxing and you're going to need that after moving."

"That's true."

"Romeo lives in Charlotte, you know."

Romeo was our good friend. Growing up it was always the three of us. While me and Romeo were always just friends, I always knew that he and Ericka could have been more. The feelings and emotions were there, even with us being young. His family moved to Charlotte when we were in sixth grade and Ericka took it hard. For college, he moved back to New York and they had a brief situation that never lasted because his plan was to always return back to Charlotte after he graduated. Mitch came into her life and she kind of just pushed her feelings for Romeo in the back.

"Oh yeah. When you move here we definitely have to have lunch together."

"Yeah. We do," she whispered.

"Is something wrong?"

"Girl, no. I'm tired and thinking about

how we're going to pull all of this off by next month."

Ericka and I had been friends for so long that I knew when she was lying. Today wasn't the day to call her out on it, so I was going to wait until she came to me. Ericka was the type that had to process things before she spoke about them. She had always been like that, and as her friend, I learned to give her space. Almost always she came and told me what she had on her mind and then we spoke about it, and I helped her process it from a different point of view.

"Okay."

"Maddie, this is the happiest that you've sounded in a while. I know Joshua was the love of your life, or so you thought he was, but this is your second chance. Allow yourself to feel and enjoy feeling that same love that you give."

"When you and Mitch get here we can

do a double date so you guys can meet," I suggested.

"I can't wait."

I heard a light tap at the door and remembered that Mari wanted to have dinner downstairs tonight. "Love you and talk to you tomorrow."

"Love you more."

I opened the door and Mari was standing in her robe. "I'm not feeling too good tonight," she coughed, and came into my room.

"Oh no... do you want to just order in and watch movies?"

Mari sat on my bed and nodded her head no. "There's no reason why you should sit and suffer because I'm sick. I called and had them keep the reservations, and the chef is going to prepare his tasting menu for you."

"You want me to sit down there and eat alone?" I've had plenty of meals alone, it would just feel weird going to enjoy myself while she was laying sick in bed.

"Yes. I don't want to ruin this trip and it's going to make me feel bad if you don't go," she stressed.

"I'm only going because I don't want you to feel bad."

Mari pulled her feet under her. "How have you and Parker been?"

"Good. Maybe too good, so I keep waiting for the other shoe to drop," I admitted. It was sad when you were so used to having things go wrong. I was the kind of person who was always suspicious when something good was going on in my life. Instead of enjoying it, I continued to brace myself waiting for the moment when it would all go to hell.

"Stop, Madison. Parker is a great guy and you're an amazing woman. You both deserve to be happy."

"What if I can't make him happy? Everything is so fresh and exciting now.

What happens when things aren't that anymore. Real life eventually takes over relationships and some ruin them."

I feared that I would end up single and trying to repair my heart for a second time. This was different than I had with Joshua. Parker had a lot more baggage than Joshua ever had, and one of those pieces was Angel. Our relationship wouldn't just be about us, it would be about Angel too. I would be a part of his life, and I witnessed how protective both Parker and Angel's mother were about their son.

"When me and Tracy started dating I was scared. Scared because I didn't know what to expect. He was always so flirtatious and fun in the office. I knew I wanted a man that would make me laugh, I always wanted a man that I could grow with too. Yes it's fun to have all the fun and energy in the beginning, but what really matters is the type of person he is when real life happens. Tracy showed me he was someone I could depend and be with when my father got sick," she paused. "He had always been goofy Tracy to me, but when my father was sick he stepped in and showed me that he could be the man I needed him to be."

"Wow."

"Stop worrying about the future and live now. Parker has a son that he has to worry about, so he's not going to rush into anything with someone he doesn't see a future with. From the way you guys were interacting at dinner that night, anybody walking by would have assumed we were all married and had been with our men for years."

"Thanks, Mari. I have a thing when I second guess everything."

"Girl, I do the same thing. Me and Tracy broke up for two days because I was second guessing if this was what he wanted. That man showed up to my house and showed me why we were meant to be together."

Tracy and Mari were so cute together. Since we've been here he had called and checked in on Mari. He even booked us a spa treatment on the day we arrived. I could tell that he was excited to get married to her. Most men didn't care about the wedding planning. All they wanted to do was show up and get married. Mari had FaceTimed Tracy and showed him the flowers and he had so much to add. He was the reason she settled on the flowers she did. It was nice to have a man's opinion at times.

"You're going to make a beautiful bride," I smiled.

"And you're going to make a beautiful bride's maid."

"What?"

"If it wasn't for you I would have been overpaying for flowers. Madison, you've been great to hang with and text. I can call you anytime and you answer."

"I am here for you, girl. Honestly... I

know how it was planning a wedding. Anything you need I'm there for you."

I opened up to Mari about my own wedding that I had to cancel. She was so sweet about it and made me laugh about the situation. Having to cancel my wedding had always been the hardest thing I've had to do. I never thought I would get to a place where I'd be able to laugh about it, and I was finally there.

"Now, go and get dressed so you can fill me in about all that good food tomorrow," she rushed me.

"Alright, alright... I'm going," I went to the closet and pulled a few options that I had packed. "Mari, seriously, thank you for inviting me on this trip."

"Girl, we need to stick together. Brookwood is a town where everything seems perfect, and we all know nothing is perfect," she winked.

Brookwood was a beautiful city that I'm sure had a bunch of secrets. From the

Pilates stay-at-home moms to the career driven ones, then you had the business men and much more. I was excited to be in a city where the majority of Black people thrived. From the way that Mari spoke, Brookwood had its own drama, and I was excited to live there so I could find out.

* * *

The Grey Goose martini kept me company while I waited for the chef to bring everything out. I was seated in a private room and I had to admit that this was the first time I had felt lonely while dining out. The whole experience was an exclusive one, or so I had been told. Even so, I wished I could be dining with the other people. Instead, I was sitting in a private room enjoying this martini while secretly wishing I was here with Parker. Other than our conversation earlier, I hadn't heard from him. He was on daddy duty, so I had to respect that. Parker had revealed how he enjoyed spending time with his son and would always choose that over anything else. So, this extra time he was getting with him was special and I didn't want to come in between that.

"Is this seat taken?"

I just knew my mind was playing tricks on me. Here I was thinking about Parker and then I heard his voice. Shaking it off, I turned around and my jaw dropped. Parker was standing there with a bouquet of blush roses in his hand.

"P...Parker," I stammered, not sure of what else to say. "What are you doing here? I...I just spoke to you earlier and you said you were hanging out with Angel."

He smiled and used his free hand to pull me out my chair. A quick kiss on the lips and squeeze of my ass, and he gently placed the bouquet into my hands. "I couldn't stop thinking about you, Maddie.

I can never stop thinking about you whenever we're not together."

"Awe, baby. I feel the same way about you. You didn't have to give up time with Angel to come and tell me this." I rubbed the side of his face and kissed his cheek.

This man made me feel so whole. It was a feeling I had never felt before. Even if I said I had, I had become so good at pretending. "I'm glad that you feel the same way... I couldn't wait another day to ask you this question."

I started to panic. Was this man about to ask me to be his wife? I enjoyed Parker and knew we could have a bright future. Was I truly ready to be engaged to him? Was he even ready to revisit that chapter in his own life? "P...Par—"

"Babe, I'm not proposing to you. We have a lot more time for that... I want us to become one before we take that step," he kissed my lips. "I want you to be my woman."

I took a huge sigh of relief. "As much as I want to be a bride, I don't think I was ready for that one yet."

"Me either. For the first time I can picture myself being someone's husband again. It's because I can see myself being your husband, Madison. I'm excited for *my* future for the first time in a long time."

"Of course, I'll be your girlfriend," I giggled and put the flowers down onto the table. "I'm going to be Parker's girlfriend," I sang while hugging him around the neck.

Parker kissed me on the lips a few times. "Nah, you're going to be my woman. My W-O-M-A-N," he spelled out.

"I have never been someone's woman before. Girlfriend, sure… never someone's woman," I kissed him again.

"Ms. Shaw and Dad kissing in the tree… K-I-S-S-I-N-G." Angel came through the door with his own flowers – sunflowers.

"Angel!" I smiled and went over to hug him. "Are those for me?"

"Yes, ma'am. You and Daddy are together now... so that means you have to pass me, right?"

"Nice try, Angel. Just because me and your dad are together doesn't mean that you'll automatically pass. It does mean that we'll get to play Uno outside of school now."

"That's a deal!" He hugged me.

Parker walked over toward us and I stood up to hug him. "Do you mind having two extra people joining your private chef experience?"

"Not at all. Mari was in on this, wasn't she?"

"She was," he smirked. "Mari believes in love, and she wanted to set this up when I told her that I was coming to surprise you."

"Maybe we can see if Angel can stay in

Mari's room tonight?" I whispered into his ear and kissed it.

Parker smirked. "Hell yeah. I'm ready to remake our first time together... I needed you, Madison."

"I needed you too, Parker Woods."

"And I needed my dad happy again," Angel smiled as we all hugged one another.

The End*
Brookwood, North Carolina has a lot more to offer. This isn't the end to Parker and Madison's story, just the very beginning of what's to come from my new series surrounding Brookwood.

Made in the USA
Columbia, SC
12 March 2023